# He wished he knew what Adley was thinking.

There had been a time, long ago, when he might have.

Four years could change a person. She was a mom now—and a widow. She had a whole host of responsibilities he couldn't begin to imagine. But that was why he'd come. To relieve some of those responsibilities, if she'd let him.

It had never been easy for Nate to open up and share his feelings, but he needed her to understand why he'd come. "I want to be here."

"I don't have money to pay you."

"I don't need money."

"You're going to work for free?" she asked, still frowning. "Is that what you had in mind? Because that doesn't make any sense— regardless of what you promised Benjamin."

"I'll do whatever you need me to do. I'll work for room and board."

She threw up her hand. "Why?"

His voice felt somber as he said, "Because I made a promise, and I'm a man of my word."

Nate wasn't about to take no for an answer. He was here to stay.

At least for now.

**Gabrielle Meyer** lives in central Minnesota on the banks of the Mississippi River with her husband and four young children. As an employee of the Minnesota Historical Society, she fell in love with the rich history of her state and enjoys writing fictional stories inspired by real people and events. Gabrielle can be found at www.gabriellemeyer.com, where she writes about her passion for history, Minnesota and her faith.

### Books by Gabrielle Meyer

### Love Inspired

Visit the Author Profile page at LoveInspired.com for more titles.

# The Soldier's Baby Promise

## Gabrielle Meyer

**LOVE INSPIRED**
INSPIRATIONAL ROMANCE

# LOVE INSPIRED®
## INSPIRATIONAL ROMANCE

ISBN-13: 978-1-335-58588-2

The Soldier's Baby Promise

Copyright © 2022 by Gabrielle Meyer

For questions and comments about the quality of this book, please contact us at CustomerService@Harlequin.com.

Love Inspired
22 Adelaide St. West, 41st Floor
Toronto, Ontario M5H 4E3, Canada
www.LoveInspired.com

Recycling programs for this product may not exist in your area.

**Printed in U.S.A.**

And hast given them this land, which
thou didst swear to their fathers to give them,
a land flowing with milk and honey.
—*Jeremiah* 32:22

To Issy, my honorary daughter
and my girls' best friend. We love you
and are so thankful you're a part of our lives.

# Chapter One

The smoke alarm sounded from the kitchen as Adley Wilson tossed the dirty diaper into the pail near the changing table. Benny began to cry as Adley scooped him up and rushed down the old farmhouse steps, holding him in her left arm as she gripped the handrail with her right hand. The last thing she needed was a fall down the steps, not with all the work she had on her to-do list today.

"Shh," she soothed Benny as she entered the kitchen and looked to the toaster where the black smoke billowed out.

With practice, Adley held the six-month-old baby in one arm while she unplugged the toaster, grabbed a hot pad to take the toast out and threw the charred bread into the sink before opening the back door to let in some fresh air.

"Oh, this toaster!" Adley said, more to herself than the baby. "It should have been replaced years ago." But where would she get the money?

Sommer, the black Lab who followed Adley all over the honeybee farm, came to the back door to see what all the fuss was about. She barked at the noise, while Benny cried even harder. Poor baby.

"Just a minute," she said to her son as she set him in his car seat and took the step stool out of the corner to reach the alarm.

Where was Grandpa Jed when she needed him? He wouldn't be able to climb the step stool, but he could entertain Benny and get him to quiet down. The eighty-five-year-old man was usually out the door before Adley even woke up, finding one reason or another to go into Timber Falls and have breakfast with his old buddies at Ruby's Bistro every morning. Adley didn't blame him. After all, he had technically retired after Adley and her late husband, Benjamin, had taken over the farm four years ago. But now that Benjamin was gone, and it was just Adley, with her limited experience, Grandpa Jed had been called upon to help more than he had hoped and planned.

But none of that mattered right now as Adley opened the smoke alarm and took out the battery.

Thankfully, the beeping stopped, but Benny was still crying, the house still smelled like burnt toast and Sommer was barking louder than ever.

Tears gathered in Adley's eyes as she picked up her baby and held him close. "This wasn't how it was supposed to be," she said as she bounced him gently. "We weren't supposed to be alone."

But there was no time to wallow in her grief. Not today. Not with the letter that had come in the mail that morning and all the work that needed to be done for the honey harvest.

Sommer continued to bark, so Adley went to the porch and found the dog's favorite tennis ball. She threw it toward the barnyard, and Sommer immediately stopped barking to chase the ball.

After Adley found Benny's pacifier, he, too, quieted, and her own heart rate began to slow. She grabbed the letter off the counter and went back to the porch where the air was fresh and she could breathe a little easier. She sat on the porch swing with Benny on her lap.

The letter was from the Minnesota Association of Beekeepers. They had received her application and she had met the basic requirements for the annual century farm grant to be awarded at the statewide beekeepers' convention the first weekend in October, just six short weeks away. As a final step in the process, the committee would be sending delegates to her farm in four weeks to make an inspection. Since the winner of the grant would also be the recipient of the Minnesota Honeybee Farm of the Year, there was a whole list of criteria the farm must meet—and that list was daunting.

Looking up from the letter, she did her own inspection of the farm. What little hope she had for the grant began to dwindle. The farm was in such disrepair, she didn't even know where to begin. Benjamin had been deployed thirteen months ago and things had started to fall apart almost from the start. But instead of returning with his National Guard unit this month, like all the others who had gone to Afghanistan, Benjamin had not come home. At least, not in the same way. Six months ago, just a week before Benny was born, Adley had learned that Benjamin had been killed in a noncombatant accident at Bagram Air Base.

He wouldn't be coming home, and the farm he had inherited from his grandfather fell further into disrepair.

"There's no way we'll qualify for the grant," Adley said to Benny as he looked up at her with his trusting green eyes. "Not with the way it looks now."

Tears threatened again, but if Adley had learned one thing this past year, it was that crying didn't solve any problems. She'd done more than her share the past six months, and she vowed not to cry in front of her son anymore. If she felt the need to weep, she reserved it for late at night, when she was alone in the room she had shared with Benjamin for the first three years of their marriage, before he'd been deployed.

A car turned off the main road and came up the driveway toward the house. Adley couldn't see it from where she sat on the back porch, but she could hear it, and so could Sommer, who started to bark. She never barked at Grandpa Jed's arrival, or even the arrival of the extra hands Adley employed during August and September to help with processing and packaging the honey. Which meant whoever had come was probably a stranger.

Adley stood and walked off the porch to stand in the yard and caught her first glimpse of the silver pickup truck. The day was hot, which wasn't unusual for the middle of August. Lake Providence shimmered in the distance, beyond the barn and the dozens and dozens of beehives. The red barn sat directly behind the house, but a large barnyard separated them. A few outbuildings filled the yard on one side, while the other was open to the pumpkin patch and the lake.

It wasn't unusual for people to stop by the farm from time to time to purchase honey or to visit with Grandpa Jed, who had lived on the farm his whole life. But it still left Adley a little uncomfortable when she was alone. Any minute, Steve and Paul, her two part-time employees, should be coming to get the morning work started. But they weren't here yet.

The pickup truck was new and shiny, and since Adley had recently needed to replace the old farm truck, she knew how expensive they could be. This didn't look like a neighbor or one of the old guys who came for Grandpa Jed.

And when the truck was closer, Adley saw it wasn't an older man at all, but someone closer to her age.

The reflection off the truck window made it hard for her to know who it was, so she waited until the truck came to a stop and the driver stepped out. He was looking away from her, toward the barn and the lake. His dark hair was cut short, almost military short. He was tall, with wide shoulders and a powerful build. He wore jeans and a plain blue T-shirt with a pair of brown work boots.

He was definitely not one of the local farmers.

When he turned and faced Adley, he slowly took off his sunglasses and met her gaze.

Adley's breath caught and her heart started to pound hard. Anger and hurt filled her chest at the sight of Nate Marshall.

"Hello, Adley," he said quietly.

"Nate." She said his name on a choked breath, all her emotions rising to the surface again, threatening to upend her right when she needed the most control.

He slowly moved around the truck and walked toward her. He looked amazing—a year of deployment would do that to a man. But it was more than that. Four years had passed since she'd last seen him, and he had grown and matured, filling out in his arms and legs and chest. For some reason, she still pictured him as the teenager from middle school and high school—but Nate Marshall was definitely all man now.

Adley swallowed the nerves that warred with her anger. Why had he come? What did he want? She hadn't expected to ever see him again.

"Is that Benjamin's son?" Nate asked, stopping a few feet away from Adley and Benny.

She held her baby closer and nodded, unable to find the words.

"He's a perfect combination of you and Benjamin."

Licking her lips, which were suddenly as dry as the burnt toast in her kitchen, Adley finally asked him, "What are you doing here, Nate?"

Nate's familiar brown eyes were filled with a myriad of emotions, many of which Adley recognized and felt herself. Guilt. Grief. Pain. Regret.

He had been Adley's friend first. When most of the other kids had written Nate off as a bad boy in sixth grade, Adley had drawn him into her circle, invited him to youth group and included him whenever possible. He'd still made some poor choices with his other friends, but whenever he'd been with Adley, he was different. Over time, he gave up his other friends and was a permanent fixture in the youth group, even getting his mom to come to church.

Their freshman year of high school, Benjamin had moved to the farm to live with his Grandpa Jed and had met Nate at football practice. Nate had been the one who introduced Adley to Benjamin, and the three of them had been almost inseparable from that day forward—at least, they had been until the day before Benjamin and Adley's wedding.

That was the day that Nate had finally confessed that he'd been in love with Adley since sixth grade but had never had the nerve to tell her.

The last thing Adley had expected—or welcomed—was learning how he felt the day before her wedding. If he had said something all those years ago, before Benjamin came—maybe things would have been different. But she had chosen her path, and she wasn't going to abandon it then. Nate's confession had put a wedge between them that had never been dealt with—one that had ultimately affected Adley and Benjamin's marriage, too. When Benjamin found out about Nate's confession, he had accused Adley of returning Nate's feelings. And no matter how much she fought with Benjamin to convince him she didn't, there was always a part of her that doubted what she was saying. But she had determined to put Nate Marshall out of her mind, to focus on her marriage and to move on with her life.

Four years ago, Adley had told Nate she never wanted to see him again.

So why was he here now?

* * *

Nate Marshall couldn't take his eyes off Adley or her baby, cradled protectively on her hip. She looked so vulnerable and alone—but she also looked angry, and he didn't blame her. He never thought he'd see her again, but he wasn't here because he wanted to be here. Not really. He'd come to the Wilsons' honeybee farm for another reason entirely.

"Benjamin asked me to come." The words fell off Nate's lips like they were easy to say, but the truth was, he'd never said anything harder in his life. He'd been practicing how he'd tell her all the way from Saint Paul, but nothing could have prepared him for how difficult it was to stand in front of her again.

To him, Adley Johnson Wilson was the epitome of character and class. She'd been one of the good girls in school, well-liked by both students and teachers. He'd been shocked when she befriended him, but it hadn't taken him long to realize that Adley saw the best in everyone—even him. He had still hung around his other friends in middle school, but after he had gotten caught shoplifting in eighth grade, and he saw how much it had disappointed Adley, he promised himself that he would never disappoint her again. She had never shamed him.

If anything, it was her unconditional friendship that had made him want to be a better person.

He had kept his promise to himself until the day before Adley's wedding—and then he'd made the biggest mistake of his life. One he was still suffering from four years later.

"Benjamin asked you to come?" Adley frowned, her green eyes filling with mistrust.

Nate nodded, playing with his sunglasses, not knowing what else to do with his hands. Guilt weighed heavily upon his heart and his conscience. He'd been with Benjamin the day of the accident, and he hadn't been able to do anything to save his best friend. The heavy cargo had fallen off the forklift as it was being moved from the plane into the warehouse. Several people had called out to Benjamin—but it was too late. Nate had been standing only five feet away, looking over the shipment list, but by the time he turned to see what everyone was yelling about, the accident had already happened.

He'd relived the scene a hundred times in his head. They'd arrived at the warehouse late because Nate had forgotten his ID back in their barracks. What if they'd gotten there earlier and been assigned to a different job? What if Benjamin had been the one looking at the shipment list, and Nate had been standing by the forklift? A thousand what-if questions had plagued him for six months.

But there was one thing that hadn't been a question, and it was what Benjamin had said to Nate as they moved the cargo off his chest— moments before he died. "Promise me you'll take care of Adley and the baby."

Nate had promised—not even realizing the gravity of his promise until after everything was said and done. But what else could he have said to Benjamin in that moment? Of course he'd take care of Adley and the baby.

So here he stood, six months later, after he was finally transitioned out of active duty, to fulfill his promise.

"It was the last thing he said to me." Nate watched her closely. She was prettier than he remembered, which was hard to believe. But more than her physical beauty, Adley had always been the kindest and sweetest girl he'd ever known. He didn't think that had changed, though he wasn't expecting any kindness from her now. Not after what he had done. "He made me promise to look after you and the baby when I came back."

Adley's mouth slipped open as she stared at him. She was dressed in a simple pair of jean shorts and a T-shirt, with her brown hair pulled back in a ponytail. Freckles were sprinkled across her nose and cheeks, and she had the longest eyelashes he'd ever seen. Even without makeup, she looked fresh and attractive. But he didn't think she'd appreciate hearing that right about now.

"I don't know why he asked me," Nate continued. "Maybe it was because I was the only one standing there who knew you—but he did ask, and I promised."

"What does that mean?" she asked, her voice and posture becoming defensive. "What could you possibly look after? Benny and I are doing just fine on our own. And we have Grandpa Jed."

Grandpa Jed was over eighty, if not rounding toward ninety. Even when they had been in high school, he had been old. He couldn't possibly be looking after the farm like he used to, though Nate wasn't about to debate with Adley. He knew she'd be defensive and angry—and proud. But he wasn't doing this for her—he was doing this for Benjamin.

"I'm here to help." Nate stopped playing with his sunglasses and grew even more serious than he had been before. He needed to try to put the past behind him, though it would be almost impossible. It had never been easy for him to share his feelings—which is why he'd ultimately made a mess of things. But he had to try now. "I'm sorry about what happened the day before your wed—"

"Don't." She put up her free hand and took a step back. "You don't need to bring it up."

He wasn't going to let this go that easily. He'd had four long years to mourn his actions and knew he had to apologize. It had been eating him alive ever since. "If there's anything I regret in my life, it was how foolish I was that day." He should never have said anything about his feelings for her. He'd been thoughtless. He knew that now. But at the time, all he could think about was how he had been secretly in love with her for eight long years and would never get the chance to tell her after she was married. Why had he finally opened his mouth the day before her wedding, though? "I shouldn't have told you. I know that now. But being here doesn't have anything to do with that day. This is about Benjamin and his dying request."

Adley bit her bottom lip as she studied him. He wished he knew what she was thinking. There had been a time, long ago, when he might have.

Four years could change a person. She was a

mom now—and a widow. She lived on the Wilsons' bee farm and had a whole host of responsibilities he couldn't begin to imagine. But that was why he'd come. To relieve some of those responsibilities, if she'd let him.

"It's out of the question," she said to him as she turned and walked toward the house.

He stayed where he was for a few seconds and then followed her, not willing to give up so quickly.

"You must have a life to get back to after deployment," she said when she came to a stop on the porch. "I don't want to keep you."

"I have a job waiting for me, but I'm not obligated to go back."

"What kind of job?"

"I'm a contractor. I was working for a large construction company in Minneapolis, but I've been wanting to break away for a long time and start something new. I have some money saved, so I have time to decide."

"Don't let me keep you." Adley went to a porch swing and picked up a piece of paper. A quick glance told him it was an official letter of some kind.

"You're not keeping me, Adley." He put one foot on the bottom step but wouldn't go any farther without her invitation. It had never been easy for him to open up and share his feelings, but he needed her to understand why he'd come. "I want to fulfill my promise to Benjamin."

"And do what?" she asked, waving the letter toward the farm, the baby still on her hip, watching his mom with wide eyes. "What is there to do? I have enough help already."

He glanced behind him. Everywhere he looked he saw work. Peeling paint, broken fences, overgrown weeds in the pumpkin patch and garden. And that wasn't even taking the house into consideration, or the fact that this was one of the busiest times of the year for harvesting the honey. After extracting the honey, they would need to process and ship it, and then prepare the hives for transportation to California for the winter. No doubt she was employing a few extra hands to help, but there were always more people needed. Nate had spent his summers working as an extra hand for Grandpa Jed. He knew a thing or two about a honeybee farm.

Nate looked back at Adley and the baby. "There's more than enough for me to do here."

"I don't have money to pay you."

"I don't need money."

"You're going to just come and work for free?" she asked, still frowning. "Is that what you had in mind? Because that doesn't make any sense to me—regardless of what you promised Benjamin."

"I'll do whatever you need me to do. I'll work for room and board."

"For how long?"

"For as long as it takes."

She threw up the hand she was using to hold the letter. "Why?"

His voice felt somber as he said, "Because I made a promise, and I'm a man of my word."

For a long time, she just looked at him. Finally she said, "You told me you'd never come back here. How's that for keeping your word?"

"That's not fair, and you know it."

A vehicle pulled into the driveway and Adley said, "It looks like my employees are here. I'm behind schedule already." She tossed the letter down on the small table by the door and pushed past Nate to greet the two older men who stepped out of a rusty pickup truck near the barn.

Nate couldn't help but notice the letterhead on the paper. *Minnesota Association of Beekeepers*. At the top were the bold words: *Congratulations, you've been selected as a finalist for the annual Minnesota Honeybee Farm of the Year.*

Adley was walking toward the barn with determined steps, so Nate took a closer look at the letter and saw a whole list of things that the committee delegates would be inspecting when they came in four weeks. One glance around the farm told him that Adley wasn't ready, but she could be, if she had the proper help.

Nate suddenly knew what he would be doing for the next four weeks—and he wasn't about to take no for an answer. Even if he had to convince Grandpa Jed, Nate was here to stay.

At least, for now.

# Chapter Two

Adley tried not to turn and look back at Nate. She was still struggling to accept that he was here. It was bad enough to see him again after what had happened, but his presence made her miss Benjamin all the more. It was strange to see Nate without Benjamin close at his side.

But beyond that, Nate reminded Adley of the guilt she felt those first few years of marriage when Benjamin's jealousy and Adley's doubts had almost torn them apart. Though things had been better before Benjamin left, after his death she'd been trying hard not to think about the early days.

"Got a visitor?" Steve Harmon asked as he reached into the truck bed and pulled out his small cooler. It was red and white and went wherever he did. Inside were his two cans of

Diet Coke, one for each break he took. His wife also put a few healthy snacks in there, hoping Steve would take his diabetes seriously— but Adley knew he hid a few less-than-healthy treats in the cab of his truck.

"Appears to be a sharp-looking fellow," Steve said.

The last thing Adley wanted to do was tell him that Nate was back. Steve and Paul Harmon had been working on the farm for years and knew Nate, but they had no idea why he had left so suddenly four years ago. They, like everyone else, thought he'd gone to Minneapolis to get a job. Adley, Benjamin and Nate were the only ones who knew why he'd really left.

Nate started walking toward the barn, and Adley knew she couldn't prevent them from knowing forever. She adjusted little Benny on her hip and said, "It's Nate Marshall."

"Nate Marshall?" Steve grinned, waiting for Nate to join them. "As I live and breathe! Where have you been, stranger?"

Nate grinned and shook Steve's hand and then Paul's. Paul was the quieter of the two brothers. He was tall and wore stained overalls. He didn't say much, but his eyes were always smiling. Unlike Steve, Paul was single. He lived with Steve and his wife on a nearby farm and had been coming to work during the honey harvest for decades.

"How are you?" Nate asked Steve and Paul.

"We're doing fine." Steve looked over Nate from head to foot. "But look at you! You must have grown a foot since we last saw you."

"I don't think so." Nate smiled, and Adley was taken aback for a minute. It had been a long time since she'd seen that smile of his. He didn't share it often—and if her memory served well, he hadn't had much to smile about growing up. His dad had left him and his mom when he was five years old, and Mrs. Marshall had worked a few jobs to provide for them.

By the time Adley had met Nate in sixth grade, when their elementary schools had joined, he had a tough exterior and was often in trouble. It didn't take Adley long to realize he was just seeking attention, though in all the wrong ways. She set out to befriend him, inviting him to youth group and to hang out with her and her friends. He still got in trouble from time to time, but by ninth grade, he had finally pulled his life together. Benjamin had been an important influence in Nate's life—Benjamin and Grandpa Jed.

"What brings you back to Timber Falls?" Steve asked, crossing his arms. He was short and wide, with a thick mustache, which he'd probably had since the 1980s.

Nate glanced at Adley, as if to see her reaction. "I've come to help on the farm."

Adley opened her mouth to protest, but Steve reached out and put his hand on Nate's shoulder.

"Great! We can use all the help we can get, right, Adley?"

"We're doing just fine on our own," Adley protested. Benny grew heavy in her arms, and he was starting to lose interest in this conversation. He began to fuss, so she put him up to her shoulder and bounced. "Nate has a job to get back to in Minneapolis."

Steve raised his bushy eyebrows. "You're doing just fine? You could have fooled me. Things haven't been fine since Benjamin left."

Adley opened her mouth to protest again, but Steve knew her too well.

"Now, don't go getting yourself all worked up," Steve said to Adley. "Things are what they are. Not anyone's fault."

"How's Grandpa Jed doing?" Nate asked as he looked around, apparently changing the subject, for which she was grateful. "Is he here?"

"He's in town." Adley adjusted Benny to her other shoulder. "Having his morning coffee with some of the men at Ruby's Bistro. He should be back soon."

"He's not doing too well," Steve said to Nate, his countenance heavy. "And he wouldn't disagree with me. It's his arthritis. Been giving him a bad time lately. He tries to help out when he can, but most days he can't do much."

"Why don't you go on and get started?" Adley asked Steve, wishing he wouldn't give so much information away to Nate. "I'll put Benny down for his nap and be out to help soon." She had a baby monitor app on her phone, hooked up to the camera in his room, so she could keep an eye on Benny in his crib. A gift from her mother, for which she was grateful.

"Need some help?" Nate asked Steve—and not Adley.

"We've got it covered," Adley said.

"We could always use your help," Steve amended. "You still remember your way around the processing room?"

"Has it changed in the past four years?"

"Not much has changed around here." Steve glanced at Adley and gave her a wink. "Except that Adley here is single again."

It took all her willpower to not roll her eyes. Steve, Grandpa Jed and even Paul, on occasion, were known to tease her about returning to the dating scene. But she'd been adamant about sticking to the farm, focusing on raising her baby and staying single. She had no wish to get married again. She hadn't been good at it the first time and didn't want to risk being bad at it again. Marriage was so much harder than she had imagined. Before getting married, she and Benjamin had almost never fought. But after their wedding, it seemed like it was all they did. And not just about what had happened with Nate, but about finances, decisions and more.

Nate glanced in Adley's direction, but instead of the teasing light she expected to see, his face was serious—even apologetic.

"You don't need to stay," she said to him.

"Come on in." Steve put his hand on Nate's shoulder, and they disappeared inside the barn, not giving Adley another chance to protest.

Paul looked over his shoulder at Adley and shrugged.

Adley shook her head, frustrated that she was outnumbered. Once Steve set his mind to something, he rarely let it go—and it appeared that he'd set his mind to Nate staying.

She returned to the house and picked up the letter on the way. She'd almost forgotten about the inspection since Nate's arrival, but there was the reminder, waiting for her.

What she hadn't told Grandpa Jed, or the Harmon brothers, or her parents—never her parents—was that she was close to losing the farm. If she didn't get the grant, she didn't think they'd be able to hold on to the farm for even one more winter. It was her last hope of avoiding failure and maintaining the property for Benny to inherit one day.

And her last hope of honoring Benjamin's memory. What would he think if he saw her now, about to lose the only home Grandpa Jed had ever known—the last link to the Wilson family legacy?

She swallowed the fear that crept up her throat at the thought.

Adley walked into the farmhouse, which still smelled like burnt toast, and set the letter on the kitchen table where she'd look at it later.

Benny was starting to nuzzle her, so she took him up to his nursery, right across the hall from her bedroom, to feed him and lay him down for a nap.

As she crept out of his bedroom thirty minutes later, she caught sight of Grandpa Jed's truck through the window. He was just pulling into the yard.

Good.

She needed someone on her side to convince Nate that they didn't need help.

It felt good to be back in the honey processing room behind the barn. Nate stood beside a stack of honey supers, which were the superstructures that held ten honeycomb frames each. These supers were placed over the hives for the bees to make wax and store their honey. The wax caps on each comb had to be scraped before the frame could be placed into the extracting machine. It was a sticky job, but it felt like home to Nate. He'd spent countless hours in this room, working alongside these men. Though it had been several years since they saw each other, they picked up right where they left off, as if they'd just worked together yesterday.

The processing room had been added on to the back of the barn when Nate and Benjamin were in high school. It was clean and orderly, with large stainless-steel honey extractors whirring and pushing honey through a long tube into vats where the honey would be stored until it could be jarred or shipped.

"Who's this young whippersnapper?" an older voice called through the noise of the machines. "Has Nate come home?"

Grandpa Jed, as he was called by everyone, entered the processing room with a grin on his face. His wrinkled skin and kind blue eyes were as familiar as this farm, and when Nate went to shake his hand, Grandpa Jed pulled him into a bear hug. It was powerful, despite his age and arthritis.

Nate grinned.

"Welcome home," Grandpa Jed said. "I was wondering when you'd be back. How was Afghanistan?"

Grandpa Jed's hands were gnarled from years of arthritis, and his face had age spots, but his energy was still evident in the shine of his eyes.

"Afghanistan?" Nate didn't even know where to begin, nor did he really want to talk about his experience. Things had settled down a lot in that region over the past decade, but it hadn't been an easy deployment. The only thing he was truly thankful for was that he and Benjamin had been there together. They'd joined the Minnesota National Guard right out of high school and were in the Red Bull unit together. They had seen each other on weekend drills but didn't communicate much outside of the guards after Benjamin and Adley were married. Being in Afghanistan together had allowed Nate the opportunity to apologize to Benjamin, and the rift between them had started to heal. It had also allowed Nate to be there at the end. "There's plenty of time to talk about all that. I'd like to know more about this grant Adley applied for—and what we need to do to make sure she gets it."

"Grant?" Grandpa Jed frowned as he looked at the Harmon brothers. "I don't know anything about a grant."

Steve and Paul shook their heads. Apparently, they didn't either.

Why hadn't Adley told them about the grant? Either she wanted it to be a surprise, or she didn't want them to know about it at all.

"Maybe I'm mistaken," Nate said, taking another group of frames out of the super and placing them into the scraping machine. "I have a lot of catching up to do around here."

"How long you planning to stay?" Grandpa Jed asked.

"I guess that depends." Nate used a handheld scraper to remove the excess wax on the edge of a frame and then cleaned out the empty super. "I was thinking about staying through the harvest." He grew serious as he looked at Grandpa Jed. "I'm sorry about Benjamin."

Grandpa Jed nodded as he looked down at the cement floor. "Broke my heart to lose him.

I've never been more thankful for this here farm—or for Adley and Benny. I don't know what I'd do without the stability the farm and my family give me." He looked up again, blinking away moisture from his eyes. "I heard you were there with Benjamin at the end. It gave me some peace, knowing he wasn't alone."

Nate was thankful that he had been there—but watching his best friend die was harder than anything he'd ever had to endure. The memory was seared into his mind and could never be removed, no matter how hard he worked or how much he tried to forget. Being back at the farm was good for him, to remember how things used to be.

"Benjamin asked me to come back here and help," Nate said. "It was the last thing he said before he passed."

"Sounds like my boy." Grandpa Jed smiled. "Always looking out for those he loved, right to the end."

"Is that why you've come?" Steve asked.

Nate nodded. He was there because Benjamin asked—but also, because he hoped and prayed there was a way Adley could forgive him. He wasn't foolish enough to think they might ever be friends again, but he hated living with the knowledge that she despised him or was still angry.

Grandpa Jed placed his gnarled hand on Nate's shoulder. "You're welcome to stay as long as you'd like. We've got a couch in the sunroom addition that no one uses. It's not ideal, but it's comfortable and air-conditioned. It'll work for now."

"You don't think Adley will mind?" Nate asked. "Because she didn't seem too thrilled with the idea of me being here."

Grandpa Jed frowned. "Adley's the sweetest thing that's happened to this honey farm—if you get my meaning." He grinned. "She'll be delighted. Besides, she loves you. You're practically family."

His words felt like a punch to Nate's gut. Adley didn't love him—might even hate him after what he'd done. But he didn't want to be the one to tell Grandpa Jed. What if he knew the truth about what Nate had said to Adley the day before their wedding? Would he be so quick to offer Nate a place to stay for the next month? Or would he want Nate to leave even more than Adley did?

The door opened and Adley entered the processing room. She paused as all the men looked in her direction—but then she closed the door and walked across the space to join them.

Grandpa Jed grinned at Adley. "Were you just as surprised as me to see Nate?"

"Probably more so," she said as she looked up at the older man. "Can I talk to you for a minute?"

"I asked Nate to stay with us." Grandpa Jed ignored her request. "He's going to sleep on the sunroom couch. I told him you'd be delighted. It does my heart good to have him back, especially after all we lost."

She didn't look delighted—on the contrary, she pressed her mouth together and took a deep breath. Adley turned her attention to Nate and said, "Can I talk to you outside, instead?"

Nate held up his sticky hands, and Grandpa Jed said, "Go wash up. I'll take over your spot for a few minutes."

"Are you sure?"

"I haven't worked in here for a long time. I could use the exercise."

Nate went to the sink and washed his hands as Adley pushed the door open and walked outside.

Before following her, Nate didn't miss the looks the three older men gave one another. The quiet, *knowing* glances.

If those three men thought they'd play matchmaker, they'd be sorely disappointed. They had no idea what they were up against.

The sun was bright as Nate left the processing room and joined Adley out in the yard. Here, at the back of the barn, they had a stunning view of Lake Providence. On Nate's left was the old basketball court he and Benjamin had spent hours on during breaks and into the evening. The cement pad had cracked in several places, with weeds growing through, and the basketball hoop had become rusted. The netting was long gone.

"How am I supposed to kick you out now?" Adley asked as she stood with her back to the lake. "Grandpa Jed will be heartbroken."

"I don't want to leave, Adley." It was true. Even though he knew it would be hard to be with her every day, to see her look at him with that anger and resentment. He couldn't leave. At least not until he helped her get the grant. He'd made a promise to Benjamin. "I made a promise and I don't want to break it."

"I was serious when I said I can't afford to pay you." She crossed her arms. "What none of them know is that this might be our last season. Right before Benjamin was deployed last summer, he invested in a lot of new machinery and another three hundred bee colonies—and I can't pay for it now. Our harvest last year was horrible, and I had to quit my job at the hospital to take care of Benny and run the farm—but it's not enough. Not close to enough."

Nate wanted to reassure her that it would be okay, but he didn't know if it would. "I don't expect you to pay me—and it'll only be until the end of the harvest." Should he tell her he saw the letter from the Minnesota Association of Beekeepers? She had already told him more than she apparently had told the others. "I saw the letter today—the one about the grant."

Adley shook her head. "I have no chance of winning that grant—but if I don't, then we're done. I can't pay for those machines, and the short-term loan will be due soon."

"But if you got the grant, you'd be okay?"

She shrugged. "*If* I get the grant—*and* the harvest is good—we might be able to pull through. But it's a long shot. I don't have the kind of money or labor force necessary to get this place put together in time for the inspection. The recipient of the grant has to have a certain image. The farm that wins will also be named the Minnesota Honeybee Farm of the Year and should be a showcase property. It'll be featured in state and national beekeepers' magazines." She motioned to the farm. "This place, as is, wouldn't stand a chance."

Nate's heart rate increased at the gravity in

her voice. In the distance, Lake Providence glistened in the sunshine. The beach where they had spent countless hours swimming and fishing wasn't too far away. It was there, the day before Adley's wedding, when they'd come out to the farm to pick wildflowers for the reception centerpieces, that he had told her he loved her. He had been the only person without a job that day and had offered to drive her out to the farm from Timber Falls—never planning to confess his love. But the moment had presented itself and he took it. He tried not to let the lake—or his memories—distract him now.

"I'm here to help," he told her. "It will be a lot of work, but we can turn this place around, if you'll let me."

"In four weeks?"

"Why not? I'm a contractor, Adley. This is what I do for a living."

Her eyes were filled with skepticism, but she finally said, "Are you sure?"

"I am. I want to do this for Benjamin—and for you."

Adley took a deep breath. "Okay—but Nate?"

"Yeah?"

"I don't want to talk about what happened between us."

It wasn't what he had hoped for, but if she

was willing to let him stay, he would agree. "Okay."

"Good." The sound of a baby interrupted their conversation, and Adley took her phone out of her back pocket to look at the screen. "Benny woke up early. It doesn't look like I'll be able to help in the processing room, after all."

"Go ahead. I've got it." He smiled at her, wishing he could do more than ease her work.

He longed to see her laugh again.

# *Chapter Three*

It was close to suppertime and Adley hadn't seen Nate since their talk behind the barn. He'd been busy all day and hadn't even come in for lunch when Grandpa Jed and the Harmon brothers had made their way to the farmhouse kitchen.

"He's still working," Grandpa Jed said with a shake of his head, though there was admiration in his eyes. "I told him I'd bring him something to eat when we're done."

So Adley had wrapped up a sandwich and some potato chips and sent them out with the men when they went back to the processing room. Then, during Benny's afternoon nap, when Adley had finally made it out to work, Nate hadn't been with the others.

"He's fogging the hives in the north pasture,"

Grandpa Jed had said. "Bringing in another load for us to process."

They owned over two thousand colonies, which were located in eighty different locations all over the county. Nate would be bringing in the last of the colonies that resided on their farm. After that, Steve and Paul would begin to bring them in from the other locations each morning when they came to work.

That evening, when the Harmon brothers pulled out of the driveway, and Grandpa Jed came into the house for supper without Nate, Adley turned from the stove where she was making noodles for chicken Alfredo. "Where is he now?" she asked.

"Getting supplies ready to fix that leak on the roof over the processing room."

"I hope you told him not to bother this evening. He's done enough for one day."

"I tried telling him, but that boy is driven. He acted like he was making up for lost time or something."

Benny was in his bouncer, happily playing with a teething ring. Adley nodded at her son. "Can you keep an eye on him while I go and speak to Nate?"

"I'd be happy to."

"The noodles will be done in a couple minutes."

"Go on," he said. "I can handle the noodles."

She knew his arthritis troubled him, but he was more capable than she gave him credit for—and he hated to be babied.

Adley opened the screen door and walked onto the back porch. Sommer was lying in the shade with her tennis ball, and the second she saw Adley, she grabbed it in her mouth and jumped to her feet. Adley threw it for her and then kept walking across the barnyard.

The old red barn was large and majestic. It had been built a hundred and twenty years ago by Cyrus Wilson, who had come to the area to farm cattle. In 1915, Michael Wilson had converted to beekeeping and had eventually become one of the largest producers in the area. For over a hundred years, the Wilson farm had survived, outlasting a depression, two world wars, and many other ups and downs. Adley couldn't be the reason it failed now—not with all the obstacles Benjamin's ancestors had overcome to keep it going.

Though the barn was large, it was full of a hundred years' worth of family treasures—at least, that's what Grandpa Jed called the junk sitting inside. The only things of real value in Adley's eyes were the tractor Benjamin had purchased shortly after they took over and the various other equipment and tools they used to operate the farm.

Since the door was open, Adley assumed Nate was inside. She stepped into the dark interior, allowing her eyes to adjust for a moment as she listened for the sound of him.

"I'm over here," he said. "Trying to find the roofing tar Grandpa Jed said would be in this corner."

Adley wanted to laugh but just shook her head instead. "I would be surprised if you found what you're looking for on the first attempt. Grandpa Jed claims he knows where things are, but it's been my experience that he does not."

Nate had been bending over as he moved things out of the way, but he stood straight now and surveyed the barn. "Ever watch that television show *American Pickers*? Those guys would have the time of their lives in here. Some of this stuff has to be as old as this barn."

"I'd love to clean this place out, but I don't even know where to start."

"Is Grandpa Jed okay with you selling some of this?"

"Selling it?" Adley hadn't even considered that. "I don't know. I'd have to ask him."

"There's a fortune to be made here." Nate picked up an old gas station sign that had been lying against a rusted bicycle. "This stuff is worth a lot of money. If you had someone who knew what they were doing, you could probably make more money than that grant is even worth."

Adley considered his words as she walked over to a weather vane. There was no way to know what was buried deep within the barn. Most of it probably hadn't seen the light of day for decades. "If I ask Grandpa Jed to sell it off, I'd probably have to tell him how bad our financial situation has become."

Nate left the sign and joined Adley near the weather vane. "Why haven't you told him yet?"

Biting her bottom lip, Adley wasn't sure if she was ready to admit the truth. As a child, her dad had always had high expectations for her, for her grades, for her behavior and so much more. She'd spent most of her life trying to meet them. She never wanted to disappoint him, or anyone else, and the knowledge that she'd have to tell Grandpa Jed the truth about their finances made her feel horrible. "I don't want him to know I failed. He's already lost so much."

"Won't it be easier to tell him now, when there's something he can do about it? Rather than wait to tell him after it's too late?"

Regret pierced Adley's heart as she thought about the truth. "I don't want to tell him at all— I'd rather get that grant and not let him worry unnecessarily. He's retired. He isn't supposed to concern himself with the farm anymore."

"Adley, he needs to know."

She shook her head. "No. He doesn't. When he worries, his arthritis gets worse. After Benjamin died, Grandpa Jed had a flare-up that was so bad, he spent three weeks unable to get out of bed. It was awful, especially because I'd just given birth to Benny. I can't risk Grandpa Jed getting that sick again." She studied Nate. "You aren't going to tell him, are you?"

Nate didn't say anything for a moment, and then he sighed. "It's not my place."

"Good." Adley remembered why she'd come out there. "He told me you are planning to work on the roof tonight, so I said I'd come and tell you to take the evening off. You've been working hard all day—and I have supper ready."

"There's a lot to be done, and I don't mind hard work." He put his hands in his pockets and shrugged. "I actually prefer it. Working is easier than sitting idle with just my thoughts for company. A man can relive a lot of poor decisions when he has nothing better to do."

For all of her frustration and anger toward

Nate these past four years, she had never stopped to consider how he had been doing. No, he shouldn't have told her that he loved her the day before her wedding, but what had it been like for him to keep his feelings to himself all those years? And why had he? That question had plagued her since the day he told her. He'd had ample opportunity to say something for years—but hadn't.

"You don't have to be alone with your thoughts," she said gently. Yes, he had hurt her, but was she going to keep holding it against him? Wasn't their old friendship worth something? "You have Grandpa Jed and Benny—and me, to keep you company now."

A slow smile lifted his lips, and he looked younger—more like the Nate she remembered from high school. He had been the strong, silent type, and there had been a lot of girls who had fallen for his charm—including Adley. But he had never said anything to her, so she had assumed he didn't return her feelings. Since he didn't date anyone, she didn't think he was interested in having a high school relationship. After he admitted the truth to her, though, she'd realized he hadn't dated because he hadn't been interested in anyone but her.

So why had he stayed silent?

The memories brought up too many unwelcome emotions, so she turned and gestured for him to follow her. "The roof can wait until tomorrow. You must be tired from a day of hard work. I put some sheets and blankets on the couch. You can bring your things in and make the sunroom your own for now. We don't use it all that much. Benjamin's grandmother had it built years ago, but it's kind of out of the way and we use the living room more."

He followed her out of the barn and closed the door.

A snazzy black Porsche pulled into the driveway, capturing Adley's attention—and making her heart fall.

"Wow," Nate said. "That's quite a car."

"It's my dad."

"Oh." The one word was all Nate needed to say to communicate his feelings about her father.

Rick Johnson was a tough man to love—let alone like. He was a self-made man; at least, that's what he enjoyed telling Adley. An investment banker, he was wealthier than most people in Timber Falls, and he loved to hold it over them. Adley had been raised with all that money could buy, in a ginormous house on the banks of the Mississippi River, in the nicest neighborhood in town. Dad had been the head elder of Timber Falls Community Church for years, until he'd had a run-in with Pastor Dawson over the new school building. Something had happened with Adley's younger brother, Aaron, but Mom and Dad had remained close-mouthed about it, and she could only guess. They still attended the church, but Dad had stepped down from the elder board. He could never have quit going. What would people think?

Dad liked to keep up appearances, thus the Porsche.

"I think maybe I'll run into the house and get cleaned up," Nate said.

"Too late." Adley lifted an eyebrow. "He's already seen you."

"Great."

Dad parked his car and stepped out in his three-piece suit. He had on dark sunglasses, and his hair was combed to perfection. He was as out of place on the farm as the beehives would be in his bank.

"Hi, Dad," Adley said as she approached him. "What brings you out here today?"

Dad was a sharp man who missed nothing. He didn't bother to take off his sunglasses, but it was easy to tell he was looking toward Nate, though his suntanned face remained impossible to read. "Hello, Adley. I came out here to talk some sense into you."

Adley wanted to roll her eyes but refrained. She loved her father, despite his tough exterior, and had been raised to respect him. So, instead, she smiled. "I've got more sense than most people, thanks to you."

"Hello, Mr. Marshall," Dad said, extending his hand to Nate. "I didn't expect to see you here."

Nate shook Dad's hand. "Just got here today."

"We've been keeping tabs on your division overseas," Dad said. "Thank you for serving."

Nate nodded.

Dad crossed his arms, all formalities out of the way. "What brings you to the farm? It surprises me that you'd be here. With Benjamin gone, it hardly seems the place for you to be hanging out."

Adley hadn't wanted Nate to stay, but she also wasn't prepared to let her father make him feel unwelcome. "Nate's working for us through the harvest. We needed the extra help."

"Can you afford that?" Dad asked.

"You don't need to worry about it, Dad."

"Where money and my daughter are concerned, I have all the right in the world to worry."

"I've got it under control."

"Nate?" Dad asked. "Can you give Adley and I a minute alone?"

"Of course." Nate didn't look like he wanted to stay anyway.

He was hardly out of sight when Dad took off his sunglasses and leveled Adley with a glare. "Both that boy and this farm are beneath you. It's time you stop this nonsense and come home to live the life you were meant to live."

His words didn't surprise her—but they made her sad.

She *was* living the life she was meant to live—even if it didn't look like the life she had always hoped and dreamed about.

Nate wasn't even in the house when he heard Rick Johnson's comment to Adley.

*Both that boy and this farm are beneath you.*

Despite being a lieutenant in the Minnesota National Guard—despite years of military training, deployment and managing a platoon—Nate suddenly felt like the poor, fatherless, troublemaking middle schooler cornered by Rick Johnson all those years ago.

"You're not good enough for my daughter," Rick had said to Nate in the hallway during their eighth-grade winter formal, just after Nate had danced with Adley for the first time.

And right after Nate had promised himself he'd never disappoint Adley again.

Nate had been getting up the courage to tell her how he felt—would have, if the song had been a little longer—and had promised himself that during the next song, he'd tell her. He'd gone out into the hallway to get a drink from the water fountain, but Rick Johnson had other plans. He had made Nate feel like he was about two inches tall and had made it very clear what he thought of him, his mother, his absent father and his recent shoplifting.

Rick had big plans for Adley—and they didn't include Nate or anyone like him.

Every time Nate had started to get up the nerve to tell Adley how he felt about her, he had remembered Rick Johnson's words, and he'd feel unworthy of her all over again.

Adley had never treated him as beneath her in any way. She didn't have it in her, which was all the more reason he had loved her. She had always looked at Nate with respect, never once belittling him for not having a father, as if it was his fault.

"I see Adley talked you into putting the work off for now," Grandpa Jed said when Nate entered the kitchen. "Supper's just about ready."

"Rick Johnson is here." Nate's words felt flat.

The only thing that made him feel like smiling was seeing the baby playing in a bouncer on the other side of the room.

Grandpa Jed looked out the window and made a face as he waved aside Nate's comment. "He won't come inside. He's never set foot in this house, and not because I haven't asked. He's probably afraid he'd soil his suit."

"He's a pretty tough man."

"As tough as they come." Grandpa Jed took the bowl of steamed broccoli off the counter and moved slowly toward the long table in the middle of the kitchen. "He gives Adley a hard time for staying on the farm. Never wanted her to marry Benjamin, but she wouldn't let that stop her."

"Where does he want her to live?" Nate asked. "Isn't this her home?"

The baby bounced and cooed, stealing Nate's attention. It was remarkable how much he looked like both his father and mother.

"Rick had other plans for Adley—I've heard him," said Grandpa Jed. "Said she was supposed to be some rich man's wife, living a life of comfort instead of drudgery. That's how he raised her."

"Isn't that line of thought a little old-fashioned?"

Grandpa Jed set down the broccoli and turned back to the stove, but Nate put his hand on the older man's shoulder to stop him. "I've got it." Nate retrieved the pasta and said, "Isn't she happy here?"

"Happy?" Grandpa Jed shook his head, sadness weighing down his already stooped shoulders as he took a seat at the table. "I think she tried real hard at the beginning, but things weren't good for her and Benjamin for the first couple of years. It didn't have anything to do with the farm, though. I think they were both surprised that marriage took work and intentionality. Things got a little better right before he was deployed and they found out they were going to have the baby. But ever since Benjamin died, and Benny was born, the guilt has been eating her alive. I don't think she's happy, but can you blame her? She's a widow, living on this run-down farm with an old codger, to boot. Not really the life a twenty-five-year-old woman would choose for herself."

Nate finished bringing the food to the table, his heart heavy for Adley. He had always wanted her to be happy. The knowledge that she wasn't hurt him deeply.

He stopped to squat down by the baby, remembering how Adley had smiled at the little guy earlier. "Benny is his name?" he asked Grandpa Jed.

"Yep." Grandpa Jed grinned. "The only bit of happiness—until you came along."

Benny stopped bouncing and looked at Nate with large, curious eyes. Drool wet his chin and shirt, and when he smiled, his bare gums showed. He was a cutie. Nate loved him all the more because he made his mama happy.

"Do you think Adley would mind if I hold him?"

Grandpa Jed shook his head. "Not in the least. The little guy loves to be held."

Slowly, Nate put his hands under Benny's arms and pulled him from his bouncer.

He was heavier than Nate expected, a solid, compact baby who fit into Nate's arms perfectly.

Benny cooed and laughed as he reached for Nate's nose. His hand was wet from drool, but Nate didn't mind.

"It's hard to think about Benjamin missing out on the birth of his son," Nate said, though more to himself than to Grandpa Jed.

"A tragedy is what it is. A boy needs a father."

Nate couldn't agree more. Though his mom had done her best and had worked several jobs to provide for them, Nate had always felt the keen loss of his dad. It made it all the harder to see Adley's father treating her so poorly— but it was a good reminder that even if a dad stuck around, it didn't mean that everything would be perfect.

The back door opened, and Adley entered the kitchen. She paused when she saw Benny in Nate's arms.

"I hope you don't mind," he said quickly.

Adley shook her head, and for the first time since he'd arrived, she smiled at him.

Nate's chest filled with warmth at that smile, even though there was still pain behind her eyes.

"You look like a natural," she said as she walked to the stove.

"We brought it all to the table," Grandpa Jed said. "Now, sit and enjoy a warm meal before that little boy of yours starts to make demands."

Adley came around the table and lifted her hands to take the baby, but Nate said, "I've got him. Why don't you sit down and eat?"

She looked from Nate to Grandpa Jed and back again. "Are you sure?"

Nate sat on the bench along one side of the long table, while Adley sat on the other side. Grandpa Jed stayed in his chair at the head.

"Shall we pray?" Grandpa Jed asked.

Nate bowed his head as Grandpa Jed's words

filled his heart and mind. The older man had been a steady influence in Nate's high school years, and his strong, confident faith still resonated. He was a father figure in all the ways that mattered, to both him and Benjamin.

When he was done praying, Nate looked up and met Adley's gaze. "Is everything okay with your dad?"

She put on a smile, though it wasn't as sincere as the last one, and said, "It will be."

Nate hoped and prayed she was right.

Now that he was here, and he saw what she was up against, he was determined to do whatever it would take to make sure it would be.

## Chapter Four

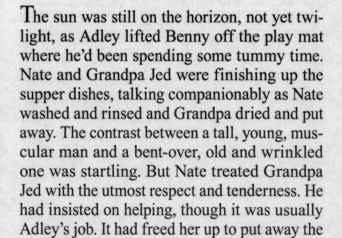

The sun was still on the horizon, not yet twilight, as Adley lifted Benny off the play mat where he'd been spending some tummy time. Nate and Grandpa Jed were finishing up the supper dishes, talking companionably as Nate washed and rinsed and Grandpa dried and put away. The contrast between a tall, young, muscular man and a bent-over, old and wrinkled one was startling. But Nate treated Grandpa Jed with the utmost respect and tenderness. He had insisted on helping, though it was usually Adley's job. It had freed her up to put away the leftovers and sweep while Benny played and she listened to the men share stories.

It was still hard to believe that Nate was back in her life, but she was even more surprised to realize how easy it felt to be around him.

Their friendship, though almost destroyed by one conversation, still had a solid foundation. It was that foundation that Adley had chosen to focus on.

Adley went to the counter and lifted a clean rag to wipe at Benny's drool—catching Nate's eye. He smiled at her as he set a clean plate into the rinse water.

Just like everything else about the farm, the kitchen was old and well loved. There was no dishwasher and no space for one. The house had been built decades before dishwashers had been invented, and Grandpa Jed and his wife had never thought to remodel and add one. When Adley and Benjamin had moved in, Benjamin had asked her if she wanted to change things, but she had loved the homeyness and warmth of the kitchen. It was the complete opposite of the uninviting, pristine kitchen at her childhood home. The farmhouse kitchen had served thousands of meals for all the Wilsons, and their friends, that had come before her. She felt honored to be a part of that tradition and didn't want to change a thing. She had quickly adapted to doing the dishes by hand, enjoying how it forced everyone to slow down, work together and visit at the end of a long day.

"I'm going to head up and give Benny a bath

and put him to bed," she said. "Do you have everything under control down here?"

Grandpa Jed hung the towel on the drying rack with a bit of a flourish and said, "We're all done, in record time. I think we have a new dishwasher to replace the old one."

Nate unplugged the stopper in the old farmhouse sink and let the water drain as he smiled at Grandpa Jed.

"Replace the old one?" Adley asked. "But I'm the old one."

Grandpa Jed shrugged, a twinkle in his eyes. "It's all about efficiency on the farm. We can't be afraid to change how things have always been done—that is, if we find a new, better way."

Adley knew he was teasing, since he, more than anyone, liked tradition. Benjamin had been the one who was trying to change things. He'd had a vision that Grandpa Jed hadn't quite accepted—which had led to all their debt. But Adley was going to change that. With Nate's help, she was going to try to get that grant. Seeing her dad, hearing him belittle her dreams, had reinforced her desire and determination to make the farm succeed.

"Need help with Benny?" Nate asked as he dried his hands on a kitchen towel.

His request surprised her. No one had ever

helped her get Benny ready for bed. Grandpa Jed hadn't been upstairs in all the years she'd lived in the farmhouse. It had been a nightly ritual she'd been doing by herself for the past six months.

"I've got it," she said.

"Are you sure?"

For some reason, his offer made tears sting the backs of her eyes. She'd felt so alone, for so long—even with Grandpa Jed in the house—that the idea of someone coming alongside her to care for Benny made her feel emotional. She forced herself to take control of her thoughts and feelings and nodded. "I'm sure."

As Adley bathed and fed Benny, all she could think about was Nate. He and Grandpa Jed had probably gone out to the front porch to watch the sunset together. They'd be laughing and talking about old times, maybe swapping war stories, since Grandpa Jed had been in the service for a short time in the 1950s.

Finally, just as the sun kissed the horizon, Benny was asleep and Adley was able to tiptoe out of his room. At this time of the day, she usually did laundry and took care of bills. Grandpa Jed often went to bed even before she finished getting Benny down.

But tonight, it was different. She wasn't even

sure she could focus on bills and housework, knowing Nate was somewhere in the house. Though what was she supposed to do? She didn't want to talk to him. It was too difficult bringing up old memories and wounds. Yet not all the memories were bad. Actually, most of them were good.

Adley turned off the stairway light as she entered the kitchen. Everything was quiet in the house, and she felt herself being drawn to the front porch. Maybe it wouldn't be a bad idea to talk to Nate and let him know her expectations. She needed to establish some sort of working relationship with him—though it might not be easy to treat him like one of the farmhands. He was so much more than that, yet he wasn't. For four years, she had tried to not even think about him.

She walked through the living room and toward the screen porch that faced west. The front door was never used by guests, since the back door opened to the farmyard and most people came in that way. Instead, the screen porch was a little sanctuary for the family. It was wide and long, extending the length of the house, and looked out over farm fields for as far as the eye could see. Trees bordered the fields, breaking up the landscape as it sloped toward the Mississippi River, not too far away.

Adley pushed open the screen door to the porch, noticing the massive riot of colors in the sky, streaking away from the setting sun.

Nate sat on one of the worn rocking chairs, his left leg hitched up and his ankle resting on the other knee.

Grandpa Jed wasn't on the porch—it was just Nate and Adley.

She started to go back into the house, not wanting to be alone with him. It was one thing to be in the same room when Grandpa—or Benny—could offer a buffer. An entirely different thing to be by herself. Nate's presence brought up so many repressed memories and feelings, she didn't know what to think. She had liked him once upon a time, but it was a schoolgirl crush. So then why had she struggled so much after he told her he loved her? Why had the truth put a wedge between her and Benjamin and made her doubt her marriage? Had there been something more to her feelings for Nate, beyond a crush? And if so, was there a chance that they could grow again, if she didn't guard her heart?

The last thing she wanted to do was betray Benjamin's memory by questioning her feelings for Nate again.

She was almost inside the house when the

old hinges on the screen door gave her away and Nate glanced up.

They looked at each other for a long moment. He was so good-looking it hurt, with his dark brown eyes and chiseled features. She suddenly wondered whether he was single, though she doubted a wife or girlfriend would be okay with him camping out on another woman's couch for so long. Yet—what did it matter? He was only here for a short time, and then he'd be out of her life again.

"Is Benny asleep?" he asked quietly.

She nodded, still holding the door open, not quite ready to commit to staying on the porch with Nate. Maybe she should just say good-night, make sure he had everything he needed and make a hasty retreat. They could talk about expectations tomorrow over breakfast.

Adley opened her mouth to say good-night, but he interrupted her.

"Grandpa Jed was tired, so he went off to bed." He looked to the empty rocker beside him. "Want to join me? There's nothing like a Minnesota sunset."

She shouldn't stay—shouldn't let herself be alone with him. It would be easier to keep a barrier between them if she stayed away, but something pulled her onto the porch and toward the chair.

Maybe it was companionship. Maybe it was for old times' sake.

Or maybe it was because she was only twenty-five years old and Nate's showing up on the farm was the most interesting thing that had happened in her life for several months.

The screen door closed behind her as she moved over the wood floor and took a seat next to him. Overhead, a fan whirred softly as the sound of crickets started to sing in the distance. A gentle breeze ruffled the leaves of the elm trees just outside the house, entering the porch to cool Adley's brow.

"I had forgotten how peaceful the farm was," Nate said gently, his voice matching the cadence of the wind as he looked out toward the horizon. "I missed it more than I had realized. Afghanistan is about as different from Minnesota as you can find on this planet."

"It has a way of becoming a part of you, doesn't it?" she mused, wrapping her cardigan a little tighter around her thin frame. In her grief, she had lost more weight than she probably should have after giving birth to Benny, making her feel colder than usual. Grandpa Jed was always chiding her for not eating like she should.

For several minutes, they sat in companionable silence. Adley was surprised at how comfortable she felt, then realized she shouldn't be. This was Nate—her friend and former confidant. They'd been through a lot. Surviving middle school together should have been enough to solidify a lifelong friendship.

"Adley," Nate said as the light in the sky gently faded. "I think we should talk about what happened."

She closed her eyes briefly, wishing he would stop bringing up the subject.

It was getting darker. Shadows danced across the lines of his handsome face. She forced herself to look away from him and take a deep breath.

"There's nothing to say." She rocked her chair back and forth. "It happened, and we need to move past it if we're going to work together."

He let out a long sigh. "I just want you to know I'm sorry."

She met his gaze again, watching the torment as it played through his brown eyes. Her heart broke for him in a way it never had before. No, he shouldn't have handled things the way he did, but she couldn't hold it against him forever. If they were going to work together, they had to find a way to lay the past to rest. And it wouldn't happen if she kept putting it off or ignoring it.

"I know you're sorry," she said gently.

"Do you forgive me?"

Adley studied him for a moment as the last of the light disappeared. She was still able to see him, but there was something about the darkness that cocooned her in safety. She didn't feel as vulnerable or exposed.

"Yes. Of course I forgive you."

A smile lifted Nate's lips, revealing a line in his left cheek that was almost a dimple.

Forgiving him didn't make everything better, but at least it was a start. If she could keep a guard around her heart and not let him back in, they might survive working together for the next four weeks.

Nate wasn't one to whistle. He'd never had much to whistle about. But as the sun came up the next morning and he stepped out onto the back porch with a cup of coffee in hand, he felt like whistling for the first time in a long time. He wouldn't whistle—but he wanted to.

Sitting on the front porch with Adley last night had felt really good, and it had been a while since he'd felt good. It still hurt every time he thought about Benjamin or the four years he and Adley had been apart because of his foolishness, but for those brief twilight minutes, he had been able to forget about everything else. He'd gone to bed with a little more light in his heart, and he'd woken up in the sunroom with energy to tackle whatever project faced him today.

Grandpa Jed's coffee didn't hurt, either.

Adley hadn't come downstairs yet with Benny. Once, sometime in the middle of the night, he'd heard the little guy wake up, crying for attention. Nate had gotten out of bed to grab a glass of water and he had heard Adley go to her son, speaking in a soft, soothing tone. Benny had quieted, recognizing his mother's voice, and then Nate had heard the unmistakable sound of a rocking chair creaking the floorboards above his head as Adley sang to her baby.

Nate had stood near the sink, in the dark kitchen, for a long time listening to her beautiful voice. His heart had ached as he thought about all she and Benny had lost, and he questioned God, as he often did, when he thought about Benjamin's death. It didn't make sense to Nate, but he resolved that he would do everything in his power to ease Adley's suffering and to make up for all that she had lost.

"Good morning," Adley said inside the kitchen, behind Nate.

"Morning, sunshine," Grandpa Jed said.

Nate reentered the kitchen and smiled at Adley when she met his gaze. "Good morning."

"Did you sleep okay on the couch?" she asked as she put Benny in his high chair.

The little guy caught sight of Nate and grinned as he babbled. Nate smiled at the baby, amazed at how comfortable he felt around him. Usually, babies made Nate nervous. He'd had no experience with them in the past, and he had always enjoyed them best at a distance. But Benny was different. Nate didn't want to watch from a distance. The child was fascinating and friendly, and for the first time, Nate wanted to experience what it was like to interact with someone so small.

Grandpa Jed was at the stove making scrambled eggs. He had already set a plate aside, and he handed it to Adley. She tested them with the backs of her fingers and then put a few small chunks on the table of Benny's high chair.

The baby immediately reached for them and grabbed a handful, which he shoved toward his mouth with glee.

Adley was watching Nate for his response, so he said, "The couch was fine. Thanks. Much better than the barracks at Bagram Airfield."

Soon they were sitting down to eat. Grandpa Jed said a prayer, and then they dug into the meal.

"Why didn't you go to Ruby's Bistro this morning?" Adley asked the older man.

"And miss my first morning with Nate?" Grandpa Jed smiled. "Ruby's can wait for another day."

"Do you usually go there for breakfast?" Nate asked.

"Almost every morning since he retired." Adley smiled. "He and his friends are some of the worst gossips in town."

"Hey, now," Grandpa Jed said. "That's not true. We're bearers of local news—not gossips. We're keeping the old ways alive. None of this new, fandangle online media stuff for us."

"Social media," Adley supplied.

"Yeah." Grandpa Jed gave a decisive nod. "You all choose to spread your news on social media, but we prefer to share our news face-to-face like our ancestors have been doing for centuries."

"I remember seeing some old newspapers in the attic," Adley said. "Back around the turn of the twentieth century there were social columns that remind me a lot of Facebook. So-and-so went to Minneapolis this past weekend to go shopping. So-and-so entertained friends from Bemidji this past weekend. So-and-so took a train to Fargo to celebrate their fortieth wedding anniversary." She took a scoop of scrambled eggs and put it on her plate. "Nothing is new under the sun. Just different."

"Listen to the girl," Grandpa Jed said to Nate with a wink. "Talking like she knows something."

Adley chuckled and shook her head at him.

Nate sat quietly watching their interaction, realizing how much he had missed the simple joys of a shared family meal. Grandpa Jed had always made him feel like he belonged, and he still felt that way.

They ate for a few minutes, their smiles fading, and then Adley said, "It's Friday, so I'm planning to make some deliveries this morning. Grandpa, can you keep an eye on Benny for me?"

"Sure thing." Grandpa Jed reached over and wiped a bit of scrambled egg off Benny's cheek. "He and I have a standing date on Fridays. You don't have to ask each week. I know the drill."

"I just wanted to make sure you're up to it." Adley's concern for Grandpa Jed was evident in the way she studied him, probably trying to figure out if he was in pain today.

"I'm great," Grandpa said. "Nate's making me feel young again."

"I am?"

"You're reminding me of the good ol' days." He grinned. "You should help Adley with her deliveries."

Nate had been planning to start working on the farm repairs, but he would much rather spend the day with Adley. He remembered making deliveries in high school. They often required a lot of heavy lifting. Maybe Adley could use his help.

"Mind if I join you?" he asked her.

Adley started to protest, but Grandpa Jed grinned and said, "I've been wanting to help her, myself, but these old hands don't work like they used to, and Benny here would be so disappointed if we didn't read the funny pages together."

"I've been doing just fine on my own," Adley said.

"But you could use the help," Grandpa Jed amended. "You know that as well as I do."

"I make do."

"Well." Grandpa Jed shrugged. "Now you don't need to."

Adley met Nate's gaze. Her green eyes were

so beautiful—yet the sparkle and joy he'd always seen in them had been snuffed out, and it made his chest ache with regret and grief. What would it take to return the shine? Could it be done? Could he do it? Or would it take someone else?

He really wanted to try.

"Do you want to come?" she asked.

"I'd love to."

Adley looked a little leery, but said, "Okay. We'll need to load up the honey first. I'd like to get going as soon as possible."

Nate stood and took his empty plate to the sink, where he began to wash it. "You got it, boss."

Adley also stood and took Grandpa Jed's plate off the table, wrinkling her nose. "No need to call me 'boss.'"

"You got it, boss." He smiled as she playfully nudged him.

It almost felt like old times. Today was going to be a good day.

Thirty minutes later, they were in the pickup truck, heading north toward Timber Falls. Nate had offered to drive, and Adley had been happy to let him. It gave her an opportunity to look over the list of distributors on her clipboard.

"Let's stop at the bakery first," she said. "See if they need to replenish their supply."

It was still early and cool enough for Nate to roll down the window. The country roads were flanked by cornfields, pastures, streams, and an occasional lake or pond. It was a quick ten-minute trip into Timber Falls as they passed over the bridge spanning the Mississippi River. The river was narrow here, near the headwaters, and low at this time of year.

Nate inhaled the scents and sights of the countryside, thankful he was done with his deployment and not eager to return to Afghanistan any time soon. It felt good to be home—to be next to Adley again, to return to his roots.

He glanced at her. She had rolled down her window as well, and the wind was blowing her brown hair all around her shoulders as she looked at her list. She was wearing her hair down today. It was wavy and thick, as silky-looking as it had always been, though it was darker than he remembered. Freckles danced across her nose, and her mouth was wide and full. He couldn't help but think about how much she used to smile.

Today she wore a pair of skinny jeans and a flowing blouse with a pair of sandals. She'd never been one for a lot of jewelry, and he noticed now that all she wore was a single gold band on her left ring finger. At one point, Benjamin had given her a large, shining diamond—one he couldn't afford at the time but had made payments on. Nate wondered why she didn't wear it anymore—and how long she would wear the wedding band.

Adley glanced up at him and met his gaze, then she looked down at her hand and spun the gold band.

Neither one said anything as Nate continued to drive into town.

He needed to remember that no matter how much he had loved Adley—or how much he might care for her still—her heart belonged to someone else. Someone Nate would never betray again.

## Chapter Five

Timber Falls was buzzing with activity when Adley and Nate pulled into town. Adley pretended she was still looking over the list as Nate parked in front of the bakery. The truth was, she hadn't been paying much attention to the piece of paper at all. It was hard to concentrate with Nate beside her, glancing at her from time to time as the wind blew through the cab, and he looked so handsome with his dark sunglasses. She doubted he even knew how good-looking he was. Nate had never been vain or preoccupied with his appearance. His style had always been clean-cut, yet simple. The National Guard had been good for his physique, though she was trying desperately not to notice.

When she had caught him looking at the gold band she still wore, it had been exactly what she needed to remind herself that her thoughts were headed in the wrong direction. Romance, especially with Nate, would only complicate matters. She wore her wedding band as a reminder that she had a responsibility to Benjamin's memory and to his child, his family farm and his grandfather. She couldn't betray him by noticing how handsome his best friend was, especially when that best friend had been the reason the first few years of marriage had been so hard.

It hadn't taken Benjamin long to realize something had happened between Adley and Nate four years ago. When he asked her, she had been honest. Benjamin had been livid—and rightfully so. Yet it was more than his anger at Nate. Benjamin had accused Adley of having feelings for their friend—and Adley hadn't been able to deny it. How could she, since she'd always loved Nate, in one way or another? Despite her doubts, she had tried to assure Benjamin that she had made a commitment to him and she would never, ever dishonor that promise. But it wasn't enough.

The first few months of their marriage hadn't been the honeymoon either one of them had hoped or expected. Tension and conflict had dimmed each day together. What made it worse was that Adley was afraid she had made a mistake—that she had chosen wrong—and that she would live to regret it. Yet she was determined to honor her wedding vows. It had taken a long time to rebuild the trust between them. When things had finally started to feel like they had a chance and they'd learned about her pregnancy, Benjamin had been deployed. Then he had died. Guilt had plagued Adley for all those wasted years, for all the pain she had brought to her marriage and for the ways Benjamin had mistrusted her.

Adley spun her wedding ring on her finger again, reminding herself that she didn't deserve another chance at a happily-ever-after, especially not with the very man who had made her second-guess her decisions.

The Timber Falls Bakery was housed in a two-story brick building on the corner of Broadway and Second Street. A unique mural had been painted on the side by a local artist, depicting the history of Timber Falls. Large plate-glass windows and a striped awning extended out over the wide sidewalk, brushing against the green lamps lining the street.

Vehicles drove by, and pedestrians strolled past the buildings on the opposite sidewalk. The sun was already baking the pavement, and the humidity had risen since they'd left the farm.

"Wow," Nate said as he parked the truck and looked up and down Broadway. "Not much has changed in four years, has it?"

"There's a new ice cream shop, and the antique store moved."

Nate smiled at her. "Like I said, not much has changed."

She returned his smile, loving that their hometown was steady and predictable. She was happy that Benny would grow up here, too.

Even before Nate opened the bakery's front door, Adley could smell the fresh-baked bread and pastries. The aroma emanated from the building in a delicious cloud of flour and sugar.

"Mmm," Nate said as he put his hand on his stomach. "I'd know that smell anywhere."

"Remember when we rode our bikes here during the summer after sixth grade and bought those character cookies?"

"The blue dye stained our tongues and teeth for hours."

"And then we rode down to Maple Island Park and tried to scare the other kids with our blue mouths."

"It didn't work."

"No." Adley grinned. "But we had fun trying."

He opened the door, and they entered the bakery. A line of customers waited for their turn to place their order. It would be a while before Adley could talk to the manager, but it didn't matter. She went to the honey stand to see if it needed replenishment.

Nate followed close behind, saying hi to someone he must have recognized.

Even before they reached the stand, Adley knew something wasn't right.

There was plenty of honey—but it wasn't all Wilson honey.

Frowning, Adley picked up the cute jar, complete with a gingham fabric cover and a piece of raffia string. The label was also cutesy, much more creative than the simple black-and-white label the Wilson family had been using for as long as she could remember.

And when she looked at the price tag, it was substantially cheaper by the ounce than hers.

"That's not your honey," Nate said, picking up a jar. "Who owns Sweet Basil Honey Farms?"

Adley shook her head, looking over the label. "It says they're based in Long Prairie."

"Long Prairie?" Nate frowned. "But that's not local."

"It's only thirty miles away—local enough." Adley set down the jar, her heart falling. "I've never even heard of them before." She pointed to a spot on the label. "But they have the Minnesota Association of Beekeepers stamp of approval. I wonder if Sweet Basil has hit all my other distribution outlets."

"Even if they have, you still sell the majority of your honey in bulk to major distributors, right? Don't you send it in fifty-five gallon drums to Iowa—or Nebraska or something?"

"Sure, but my local sales are a nice chunk of income. I can't afford to start competing with another farm. Especially one that clearly has a better handle on marketing." She picked up the jar again. "Look at this. It's adorable—and less expensive than mine."

Nate shrugged. "So change your packaging." He held up one of the Sweet Basil jars next to the Wilson Honey jar. "If you didn't know that Wilson honey was superior to all other honeys—" he grinned "—and you were only making your purchase based on appearances and cost, which one would you choose?"

Adley bit her bottom lip, obviously knowing the answer. She had wanted to change things when she first came to the farm, but she hadn't wanted to step on Grandpa Jed's toes. Since Benjamin died, she hadn't given it much more thought.

But it was clear that she would have to start thinking about it, and fast. Most of the Wilson honey she had dropped off last week was still on the shelf.

"If Grandpa Jed is the problem," Nate said, reading the situation better than she had realized, "you just need to be honest with him and let him know things aren't going as well as you'd like. Maybe it's time to make a change."

Dread pooled in her gut at the idea of having that conversation. Grandpa Jed didn't scare her—but disappointing him did. What if he took offense at her idea?

"Come on," Nate said, nudging her. "Where's the courageous girl who used to stand up to bullies on the playground and crush it on the volleyball court? You're a single mom, running a business and a farm with only a few years of experience. You can handle a hard conversation with Grandpa Jed."

Adley took a deep breath and set the honey back on the shelf. "Maybe you're right. If I don't make some changes soon, we won't have a farm to worry about."

"Exactly." Nate put back the honey he was holding, his face becoming pensive. "Where else do you distribute locally?"

She gave him a quick rundown of the spots

she distributed to in the area. The grocery store, a few gift shops, the meat market and, strangely enough, the tractor supply store.

"You make a large portion of your income from those few locations?" He lifted his eyebrows.

"Everyone in town knows where to get their honey. I don't need a lot of locations—but if people have other options..." She motioned to the Sweet Basil honey. "I will need to step up my game." The very thought made her feel exhausted. She was barely treading water as it was. How was she supposed to find a reserve of creative energy for marketing?

"I'd love to help, if you'd let me."

"Do you know something about marketing?"

"Actually, I do. Before I got my contracting license, I was thinking about going into marketing. I took a few classes at the University of Minnesota, including some design classes. I'd love to play around with some packaging and distribution options—if that's what you and Grandpa Jed want."

Adley almost cried in relief. The weight that was lifted off her shoulders was immense. "I'd love that, but maybe we should wait to talk to Grandpa Jed until you have the new designs in place. It would be easier to get him on board if he could see our vision."

Something warm and sweet entered Nate's gaze, and Adley felt it herself. She loved brainstorming with him. She'd missed Nate more than she realized, and it was nice to be dreaming and scheming with him again.

"Should we go and see what other damage Sweet Basil has caused?" Adley asked.

"Sure."

They left the bakery and walked toward the pickup. Adley glanced at him again. He smiled at her, and in that moment, she realized that perhaps God had sent Nate right when she needed him most.

She wasn't sure what to think of that idea.

It took several hours, but Nate and Adley made the delivery rounds. Everywhere they went, they found the Sweet Basil honey. Adley told Nate that she had only replenished about a third of the amount she usually did on Fridays.

Nate suggested that they check with the local restaurants and see if they'd be willing to buy their honey from the Wilsons and be able to claim locally sourced honey on their menus. A few placed orders, and it prompted Nate to suggest that they drive out to some of the surrounding resorts in the area, as well.

They stopped for a quick lunch at a lakeside

restaurant that was teeming with summer tourists and then went to all the resorts they could think of in a thirty-mile radius of Timber Falls.

The heat had continued to rise, and the humidity had become oppressive. Nate wiped his brow as he slid a box of honey back into the bed of the pickup truck as they finished doing business with the last resort on their list.

Adley accepted the resort owner's check and then met Nate at the truck.

"Good thinking, Marshall," she said as she closed the truck's gate. "I exceeded my weekly sales with your suggestion."

"Thanks, Wilson," Nate said with a lopsided grin. "I have a few good ideas from time to time." He nodded toward the south where a dark wall cloud had appeared in the past ten minutes. "Looks like we need to head back to the farm before that hits us."

Adley turned to look where he was indicating. Concern tilted her brow as she nodded and then walked around the truck to get into the passenger side.

Nate jumped into the driver's seat and started the engine. He turned the air-conditioning up as high as it would go, his skin slick with perspiration and humidity.

With bright red cheeks, Adley waved her

clipboard in front of her face. "I didn't realize
it was going to get so hot today."

"That's August in Minnesota for you." Nate
pulled out of the resort, a little jealous of the
guests who were lounging around cabins and
swimming in the nearby lake. "Do you still
swim at the little beach on Lake Providence?"

"I haven't been down to the beach in years."
Adley adjusted the vents in the truck so the ones
closest to her would blow on her face. "Last time
I was down there was probably—" She paused
and then said, "The day before my wedding."

The day Nate told her he'd been secretly in
love with her for years.

"Remember the bachelor and bachelorette
parties meeting up there?" Adley asked, clearly
trying to change the conversation. "That was
a fun evening."

Nate hadn't thought about that night for a
long time—not because he didn't want to, but
because he knew he shouldn't. It had been the
week before Benjamin and Adley's wedding,
and Nate had been miserable, knowing in seven
short days he would lose Adley forever. He'd
almost told her how he felt that night, but had
chickened out, like all the other times. Instead,
he had watched her shining bright, as happy
as he'd ever seen her. She and Benjamin had

stayed close to each other that evening, and Nate had been one of the crowd there to witness their joy. He'd been a fool to think he had a right to say anything to her.

Then or now.

They were thirty miles north of Timber Falls and had a forty-minute drive ahead of them. Nate got on the road, watching those clouds building faster than he liked.

"What does the radar say?" Right as he asked her, both of their phones dinged and a weather-alert statement popped up.

Adley opened the app and read the message from the National Weather Service.

"It doesn't look good. We're in a thunder-storm warning and a tornado watch until seven this evening."

Nate glanced at the clock. It was only three.

"The radar is showing a pretty significant cell, and the farm is in the direct path." She bit her bottom lip for a moment. "I'm going to call Grandpa and make sure he's aware."

Her hands were shaking as she pressed a few buttons. They both waited silently as the phone rang. Adley's eyes were growing more and more concerned as she watched the storm clouds build.

"He didn't answer." She swallowed hard. "He hasn't been in the basement in years. I don't even know if he can get down there on his own. What will he do if there's a tornado and he needs to get Benny to safety? There's no way he could do it." She put her hand to her mouth, panic in her voice. "I never even considered a scenario like this. He's always been so good with Benny, helping out whenever he can. It's easy enough for him if they stay on the main level. I have a Pack 'n Play that Benny sleeps in, and Grandpa can pick him up and move him around as much as he needs to. But how will he get him down those stairs?"

She was becoming more and more terrified as she spoke. Her face had gone pale, and she was now shaking all over.

Nate reached over and gently took her hand in his. She latched on to him and held him tight.

"It's going to be okay, Adley." He tried to speak as gently as he could over the hum of the vents. "The farm has been standing there for over a hundred years, and it hasn't blown away yet."

She swallowed and nodded as she studied him, and he could see she was grasping for something solid to cling to. She needed him to keep reassuring her.

"Grandpa Jed is a smart guy. He'll know how to handle the situation. He's been through a lot scarier times, and he's always come out on the other end." Even as he spoke, Nate was praying for their safety, hoping that the storm wouldn't cause any damage and Grandpa Jed wouldn't have the need to go into the basement.

"Can you hurry?" she asked him.

"Sure." He put more pressure on the pedal, aware of the speed limit but anxious to set her mind at ease.

For several miles, she clung to his hand. He was conscious of every single moment, almost holding his breath, afraid to move or do something that would make her realize what she was doing.

He liked feeling needed, especially by Adley.

The wind began to blow, and the sky started to darken as the wall cloud moved even closer, blotting out the sunshine.

They came to a country intersection, and as Nate pressed on the brakes, Adley suddenly let go of his hand, as if finally realizing she was holding it.

He glanced at her and she met his gaze, but made no move to apologize or explain away her behavior. He wouldn't have wanted her to.

Adley's phone began to ring and she grabbed it, fumbling with it for a moment as she slid over the small icon on the bottom and put it up to her ear. "Grandpa?"

Nate continued to drive toward home, watching the clouds closely. There was a strange greenish hue spreading over the land, and suddenly he wasn't just concerned for Grandpa Jed and Benny. What would he do if he and Adley were caught in a tornado or strong storm on the road? It would be far more dangerous for them to be out in the elements than for Grandpa and the baby to be in the house.

"Yes," Adley said to whatever Grandpa Jed was saying. "Okay. I understand. Yes, we'll be careful. Thank you. I love you, too. Kiss Benny for me."

She hung up the phone and let out a long breath.

"Everything okay?" Nate asked.

"Grandpa and Benny are in the bathroom on the main level. It's an interior room without windows. He said Benny is sitting in the dry bathtub with some of his toys, having the time of his life. They'll ride out the storm in there, but he wants us to be careful and pull over if we need to take cover."

They were on an open road with cornfields all around them. There wasn't anywhere to take cover. He'd heard somewhere that if a person was ever caught outside in the path of a tornado, they should lie down in a ditch, because tornados tended to jump ravines and ditches. But there wasn't even a ditch that he could see.

The wind blew hard against the truck as Nate pushed them on.

Both of their phones lit up a second before a loud beeping noise blared.

Nate's heart rate picked up speed, and he started to sweat for an entirely different reason.

"It's a tornado warning," Adley said as she read the message on her phone. "There was one spotted west of Timber Falls, heading northeast."

Right into their path.

"What do you want to do?" Nate asked her.

"I don't know." She clutched her phone as she looked out the cab windows. "There! I see a farmhouse."

He saw it, too. It wasn't too far off the road and looked clean and welcoming. The farmhouse was a perfect square with white siding and a third-floor dormer window. It appeared to have been there for many, many years, with mature trees, a thick foundation landscape and several outbuildings.

"Should we see if they'll let us take cover with them?" Adley asked.

"I don't think we have a choice."

The wind was whipping so hard now, Nate was struggling to keep the truck on the road. Rain started to fall in huge drops, and then quickly it was downpouring to the point that

Nate could hardly see the road anymore. Hail soon followed, pounding against the truck's hood and roof. It was so loud, Nate couldn't hear Adley when she said something.

"What?" he asked above the wind and rain and hail.

"There's the driveway," she shouted back as she gestured to the right.

Overhead, the clouds were swirling—yet hovering in a strange dance. Nate wondered where the tornado had gone. Was it still on its way toward them? How soon might they see it?

Carefully, he pulled off the road and onto the driveway. The hail was so intense, it was denting the hood of the truck, and he was afraid that if they didn't find cover soon, it would start to crack the windshield. He could no longer see the farmhouse, but he knew it was there—somewhere. He was thankful they had seen it before the rain started, or they might not have even known it existed.

He drove up the driveway, and finally, the house came within sight. There were no lights on within—and no cars in sight. What if the people weren't home and the doors were locked?

Nate hated approaching a stranger's house—not only because of his and Adley's safety, but because he didn't want to scare some unsuspecting farmers. But there was nothing else for them to do. The tornado warnings on their phone continued to blare, and the force of the wind had changed. It now sounded like a ferocious beast had been unleashed. It howled like it was coming down the length of a long, narrow tube.

Nate quickly parked the truck. "Come on—we need to make a run for the house. Try to cover your head as much as possible from the hail."

The moment Nate turned off the engine, Nate and Adley leaped out of the truck. Nate met her at the front and took her hand, using his other one to shield them as best as he could—though it was more of an instinctual gesture and was completely useless against the fury of the storm.

Hail hit them as they ran to the covered porch at the front of the house. It was painful, but they didn't have any choice. Their feet slipped on it as it covered the ground like snow. When they reached the porch, it offered them protection, and Nate stopped for a moment to check if Adley was okay.

She was drenched from head to toe, her hair

hanging around her as water dripped from the clumped strands.

"Are you okay?" he asked.

"Yeah. You?"

He nodded and then turned to the door. Even if he knocked or rang the doorbell, would they hear him inside? The storm was so loud that he doubted it. But could he just walk into their house?

The rain and hail and wind suddenly went still, as if all the air had been sucked out of the sky. White hail lay everywhere, but Nate hardly had time to notice it when he saw the funnel cloud, dipping from the sky over the road they had just left moments ago.

He didn't wait, didn't pause, didn't even think, just opened the front door of the farmhouse and pulled Adley through.

It was dark as they stood in the entryway. The house smelled like lemon polish and old furniture.

"Hello?" Nate called as he closed the front door. "Anyone home?"

No one answered him.

"We need to get into the basement," Adley said.

"The stairs are probably in the kitchen." He

led her through the entry toward the back of the house, assuming the kitchen would be there.

It was a beautiful home, well cared for. As they walked through, they kept saying, "Hello! Anyone home?"

Finally, they found the kitchen, and sure enough, there was a door that looked like it went into a basement. Nate opened it and found the stairs. It was dark, but a flashlight appeared at the bottom, though it was hard to see who was holding it.

"We're sorry to barge in on you," Nate said. "We were on the road and needed somewhere to take shelter."

"No need to explain, son," came an older male voice. "Come on down and wait it out with me and the missus. Electricity went out, but we have candles and flashlights."

Adley held on to Nate's hand so tight it hurt, but he wouldn't let her go. He'd been in stranger situations in his life, especially in Afghanistan. He was a big guy—probably more alarming to the occupants of the house than they were to him. He could take care of Adley, no matter who was in that basement.

A strange, howling sound filled the air as the windows in the kitchen rattled. Nate led Adley down the old rickety stairs and into the basement. It was musty and felt a bit damp, but it was the safest place they could be right now.

The gentleman with the flashlight kept it on their feet until they were in the safety of the basement. The house was so old, the foundation was made of rocks and the floor was dirt.

"Look what the storm drug in, Ma," said the man. "A couple of strangers."

"They won't be strangers for long," an older woman said as the man flashed his light toward him and his wife. They looked like they were as old as Grandpa Jed—and about as threatening as a pair of houseflies. The man was wearing bib overalls, and the woman was in a floral housedress. "Come on in and make yourselves as comfortable as you can while we wait this thing out."

Nate and Adley found a place to sit on a large wooden box. He put his arm around Adley and held her close. She was shivering, so he ran his hand up and down the length of her arm to warm her.

"Thank you," Adley said to them. "We feel horrible for coming in uninvited."

"It's no problem," the man said. "What are neighbors for?"

"What're your names?" the lady asked. "I'm Stella and this is Hank. Westermann is our last name."

"I'm Adley Wilson," she said. "And this is Nate Marshall."

"Jed Wilson's granddaughter?" the man asked.

"Yes." She wasn't really his granddaughter, but for all intents and purposes, Nate supposed she was.

"We missed him at Ruby's this morning," said Hank. "When you see him, tell him he still owes me a cup of coffee."

Adley glanced up at Nate, and a small smile tilted her lips. "He'll be happy to hear that."

As the storm raged above them, Nate and Adley sat in the cool basement and made new friends.

Nate loved being back home—but he loved how close Adley was sitting next to him even more.

# Chapter Six

It felt like the storm lasted for hours, but within twenty minutes, Adley and Nate were back in the truck, heading toward home as fast as possible.

"I can hardly believe the damage," Nate said in a hushed tone as he took in the landscape all around them. "But it could have been so much worse."

Adley was silent as she surveyed the mess, her heart still pounding hard. Tree branches were strewn everywhere, cornfields were flattened, and several of the homes and barns they passed were missing parts of their roofs. But Nate was right. So far, nothing looked like it was totally lost. Thankfully, the Westermanns' home had sustained very little damage, just a tree branch down in the front yard.

"From what I can tell," Nate said, "the storm went directly toward your farm. It looks like it followed the road we're on, almost perfectly, but it must have lessened a bit."

It took everything within Adley to stay where she was seated as she clutched the door handle. If she'd been driving, she would have been reckless to get to Benny and Grandpa Jed.

"Did you try calling Grandpa again?" Nate asked.

"No answer." Adley licked her dry lips, hoping and praying that nothing had happened to Grandpa Jed or Benny.

"Maybe his battery died or he has his ringer off."

Adley appreciated that Nate was trying to make her feel better. So far, he'd put her mind at ease all throughout the storm, constantly reassuring her. But now, as she saw the damage it had done, she wasn't so easily calmed.

It took another twenty minutes to get home, and as they pressed on, the destruction to the surrounding area continued to alarm her. Thankfully, it didn't look as if there were homes or buildings destroyed, but they were definitely affected by the strong winds.

Adley strained to get a glimpse of the house and barn on the Wilson farm.

The first thing she saw was a huge oak tree that had partially come down in the front yard. A large branch was ripped off the trunk and was lying on the ground. Just beyond that, the house stood, strong and solid. A few of the shingles had been torn off, but other than that, it looked secure.

"Thank You, Lord." Adley breathed a sigh of relief as she said a prayer. "The house looks secure."

The driveway was littered with tree branches, forcing Nate to drive on the grass to get around the house to the back. But when he did, Adley saw the damage to the barn. It hadn't fared as well as the house. A few sections of the roof had blown off and were lying in the pumpkin patch, exposing the contents of the barn to the elements.

"It's a good thing I didn't waste my time fixing the leaking barn roof today," Nate said. "Would have been a waste of energy."

She knew he was trying to lighten the mood, but all Adley could think about was getting to Benny.

When Nate pulled the truck to a stop, she jumped out, leaving the passenger door open as she ran toward the house, up onto the back porch and into the kitchen.

"Grandpa?" she asked, breathless as she rushed through the kitchen and into the bathroom.

They weren't in the bathroom, though some of Benny's toys were still in the dry bathtub.

"Grandpa?" Adley shouted again, her heart pounding so hard it made her head ache. As she left the bathroom, she met up with Nate, who had come into the house.

"Did you find them?"

She shook her head as she rushed into the living room. "Grandpa?"

"We're out here, surveying the mess." His voice carried to them from the front porch.

Adley's relief was so profound, her knees grew weak.

Nate was there, and he put his hand under her elbow.

She looked up at him, his steady presence reassuring her, yet again.

They walked out to the porch and found Grandpa Jed sitting on a rocking chair with Benny asleep in his arms.

"No sooner did we get out here," Grandpa Jed said, "than the sound of the dying storm put him right to sleep."

Adley wanted to rush to her baby and pull him into her arms, but Grandpa Jed looked comfortable and so did Benny. She loved knowing that her son felt safe and secure with him.

"It could have been so much worse," Grandpa Jed said to Adley. "So much worse. I'm just sitting here, thanking God He got us through another storm."

He *had* gotten them through another storm—just like all the others. Adley's heart was starting to return to a normal beat, but then she looked out at the front yard and saw more damage, mostly to the trees on the property. It would take them days to clean up—not to mention how much time and money they'd need to fix the roof.

She sank into the other rocking chair as she shook her head. "I was feeling so hopeful today when we found several new customers—but then this happened. Why do I feel like every time we take a step forward, something sends us backward?"

"That's just life, kiddo," Grandpa Jed said. "It's a constant battle to maintain your foothold. That's why you have to decide which battles to fight and which to ignore."

Nate moved across the porch and went to stand near the screen to look outside. He had his hands in his pockets as he took a deep breath and then let it out. "Sometimes the battles choose us, don't they?"

"True," Grandpa said. "There are some battles you don't have a choice to fight, like when my Clara got cancer." He paused for a moment, and Adley waited to hear if he would say something else. She'd never met Grandma Clara. Benjamin's grandmother had passed away when he was in elementary school, leaving Grandpa a widower for seventeen years now.

But he didn't say anything more. Instead, he looked past Adley and Nate toward the horizon. Even though he'd been without his wife for so long, sometimes the grief looked very fresh in his eyes.

"The battles we don't choose are often the ones that shape us the most," Grandpa finally said. "They require the hardest fights, the most perseverance and the biggest sacrifices. But at the end of the day, no matter the outcome, they're always worth the fight. Always."

Nate turned and met Adley's gaze. She had already felt like she had lost so many battles. She didn't think she had it in her to keep trying. Her marriage to Benjamin had been a fight, coming to the farm and trying to make it succeed had been a fight, and then raising her son as a widow had been the biggest fight of her life. Could she keep going?

"Do you mind if I put out a call for help?"

Nate asked her. "I have a bunch of Guard friends who would be here in a flash if I asked."

Adley opened her mouth to respond and say that she didn't want to burden anyone, but Grandpa Jed beat her to it.

"I've already had a call from Hank Westermann. He said you two took shelter in his basement during the storm." He looked at Adley. "That's why I didn't answer when you called. I was talking to Hank, and he said he'd make a few calls to let everyone know that there's a lot of damage out this way. Then I called Pastor Dawson and told him what happened. People should be arriving any minute to lend a hand."

"I don't want to inconvenience anyone." Adley hated to think that people would be changing their evening plans to come out and pick up a bunch of branches in her yard.

"Why else did God put us on this planet?" Grandpa asked. "If not to help each other out? That's the trouble with your generation. You're all 'connected,' but everyone's too afraid to be dependent. It seems like you tell each other everything, except for the hard stuff. You have all sorts of reality television, but no one's real. You're scared to look weak or in need of help, so you stand alone and fight the battles by yourself, putting on a fake smile. In my day, you didn't even have to ask. People just showed up when there was a need. There's no time on a farm for pride."

His words convicted Adley, and she reached over and put her hand on his bony shoulder. "You're right."

"I know I'm right." He smiled. "And I'm old enough to not be ashamed to tell you when I'm right."

Nate chuckled. "I'll go get started. I want to make sure the hives are okay and do a quick inspection on all the buildings."

"Are you and Benny okay in here?" Adley asked Grandpa.

"Sure enough."

"Then I'll go take a look with Nate."

She left the porch with Nate, conscious of his size and strength, remembering how much she had appreciated it as they'd raced through the storm and waited it out in the basement of the Westermanns.

When they were on the back porch, Sommer came out of wherever she'd been hiding—her tennis ball in her mouth—apparently unfazed by the harsh weather.

Nate chuckled again and bent down to rub Sommer's ears. "Good to see that she found somewhere safe to hide."

Sommer dropped her ball for Nate to throw, so he stood and threw the ball farther than Adley had ever been able to throw it for the black Lab.

"You better be careful," Adley warned him with a smile. "Once she knows you're willing to throw the ball, she'll keep coming back until she wears you out."

"I don't mind." He chuckled as he watched Sommer run after the ball. Slowly, he turned to survey the damage. Adley didn't even need to look at the farm to know they had a lot of work ahead of them. But there was no time to worry about how hard it might be, or how much time they'd waste when they should be processing honey.

Now was the time to roll up her sleeves and stop lamenting about the cards she had been dealt. If Nate was willing to help, and there were others who would soon show up, she would give everything she had left to fight for her farm. It was a battle worth all the blood, sweat and tears she had to give—just like Grandpa Jed had said.

It was amazing how quickly the farm was cleaned up after the work crews began to arrive. Nate had a hard time keeping up with all of them. No sooner was one area cleared than someone was coming up to him asking where they should work next. Not only did they clean up all the branches and debris from the trees, but they also cleaned up and hauled away the parts of the barn roof that had flown off and landed in the pumpkin patch.

More people came and suddenly, there was a group up on the barn roof beginning to make the necessary repairs. Nate didn't know where the supplies had come from, but within two hours, the roof was patched up and looked as good as new. They also dealt with the leak over the processing room that he hadn't gotten to and replaced the shingles on the house.

Adley was busy baking cookies and bringing out lemonade. She seemed to know everyone who had come to help, but if they were strangers, Nate wouldn't be surprised. She spoke to each person as if they were her dearest friends. Even Mr. and Mrs. Westermann stopped by to make sure everything was okay. Mrs. Westermann was soon inside, attending to another batch of cookies while Adley refilled lemonade glasses.

All the while, Adley wore Benny in a carrier on her back. The baby was a hit, with his big green eyes and wide, wet smile, charming even the toughest-looking farmer among them.

Nate loved watching Adley, especially when she didn't know he was admiring her. She was so good and so kind, it reminded Nate of when they were younger and he watched her with her friends at church or school, always amazed when she turned those beautiful green eyes on him and noticed him, too. It still warmed him that she considered him a friend, then and now.

By the time the sun set, all the work was done, and everyone was on their way home again.

Benny had been put to bed at some point, and Grandpa Jed was on his way there, too. It was just Adley and Nate, waving goodbye to the Westermanns as they pulled out of the driveway. Nate and Adley had promised that they'd stop by in the morning and help them with their mess, but the Westermanns said not to worry, a group had already been at their house.

"Isn't it amazing?" Adley asked Nate as they stood in the driveway, waving at the Westermanns. "Just this morning, we didn't know them, and now I feel like I have another set of grandparents watching out for me."

The sky was a riot of colors after the stormy afternoon. The air felt fresh and crisp, and the temperatures had fallen. In the distance, the reds, purples and oranges in the clouds reflected in Lake Providence, surrounded by the lush greenery of the landscape.

"Hank promised to bring over some of Stella's homemade banana bread tomorrow." Nate smiled to himself. "All I said was that I hadn't had any since I was deployed, and he jumped on the chance to give me some of Stella's."

Adley studied him in the dying light and said, "Anything else you missed while you were deployed?"

He knew she meant food-wise, but he couldn't help but think about how much he had missed her while he was in Afghanistan. How much he had missed her these past four years.

Another set of headlights appeared on the road before Nate could say a thing. Hank and Stella's taillights disappeared just as the new car turned into the driveway.

Nate almost felt smothered. It was wonderful to get the help they needed, but after a day of managing dozens and dozens of well-meaning neighbors, he was exhausted.

Adley sighed and crossed her arms. "It's my dad."

Nate's attention became alert, and he straightened his back before he started to walk away. "I, uh, should probably check on the, ah—"

"Stay?" she asked, her green eyes imploring him.

Even if Nate had been scheduled to meet with the general of the Army National Guard, he wouldn't have been able to leave Adley's side at that moment.

"Of course," he said. His dislike for Rick Johnson made him feel protective of Adley. He knew what Rick was capable of, even with his daughter.

Nate took a step closer to her. He had the urge to put his arm around her, like he did when they were in the Westermanns' basement, riding out the storm—but he didn't. In a lot of ways, facing her father was like facing an unpredictable storm—and just as dangerous and destructive.

Rick pulled his Porsche up to the house and put it in Park before he stepped out of the vehicle. He wasn't alone. He opened the back door and Adley's mother, Susan, got out. But it was the stranger who opened the passenger door that had Nate the most curious. He was a well-dressed man, probably in his early thirties, with a suave air about him.

"What is he doing here?" Adley asked under her breath as she and Nate walked to the parked car.

"Who is he?"

"One of my dad's new business partners. His name is Spencer Ford. My parents invited me over for supper a couple weeks ago and introduced us." Her voice was full of exasperation. "It's one thing to trick me into going to their home to try and set us up, another to bring him to my house."

Nate looked sharply from Adley to this new guy. Had her parents really tried to set her up?

Spencer was looking over the property with a keen eye, and when he caught sight of Adley, his entire demeanor seemed to lighten.

"Adley!" Mrs. Johnson hurried toward her daughter. She looked like she was going to wrap Adley in a hug, but at the last second, her husband's voice stopped her.

"Susan."

Susan paused and, instead, reached out and gently touched Adley on the arm, hiding her emotions behind a mask. "I wanted to rush to your side when we heard the storm came through this area, but we were detained." She glanced at her husband and lifted her chin. "Your father had a business dinner in Brainerd that we couldn't miss."

"It's okay, Mom," Adley said as she turned and acknowledged her father and then the new guy. "Hello, again, Spencer."

He flashed her a bright smile. "Hello, Adley. It's nice to see you."

"Nate." Mrs. Johnson turned her wide-eyed gaze on him. "This is a pleasant surprise."

"I told you he was here," Rick said to his wife.

"No, you didn't. I would have remembered if you said Nate was in town."

"I quite distinctly remember telling you." Rick's voice had taken a tone that suggested he was not to be questioned. "You never hear a word I say."

"Please," Adley said, clearly uncomfortable with her parents fighting in front of everyone. "Would you like to come in for some coffee?"

Rick shook his head. "We don't want to impose. We just stopped by to make sure everything was okay. Your mother was worried."

"You're not imposing, Dad." Adley crossed her arms. "I don't think you've ever been in the house before."

Rick looked toward the old farmhouse and wrinkled his nose, but then he glanced back at Adley. "We actually have another reason for our stop—it's why we've brought Spencer along." Rick tipped his head toward Nate. "Maybe a little privacy would be in order for this discussion."

Nate stiffened, but he looked at Adley to see

what she wanted him to do. Maybe, with her mom present, she didn't need Nate.

But when Adley met his gaze, and he saw the discomfort behind her eyes, he knew she wanted him to stay. So he did.

Adley's back straightened. "Whatever you have to say, you can say it in front of Nate."

"This is a private family matter," Rick said.

She took the smallest step closer to Nate. "Nate's practically family."

The simple three-word sentence filled Nate with the most indescribable feeling he'd ever experienced. Warmth, hope and a sense of belonging. He'd never felt anything like it before.

Rick pressed his lips together. "Fine. It's about the farm. Spencer found a buyer."

"A buyer?" Adley frowned. "But the farm's not for sale."

"Everything is for sale," Spencer said with a pleasant smile. "At the right price—and the buyer is willing to offer far more than this farm is worth."

Adley looked from Spencer to her father, as if she was trying to unravel some sort of puzzle. "Why would you think this farm is for sale?"

"I knew you'd never leave of your own accord," Rick said. "So I told Spencer to look for an investor. He found someone in the Twin Cities who needs a country getaway. They're looking for a nice fixer-upper with potential. I told him this farm has potential, if nothing else."

"It's loaded with potential," Spencer agreed as he looked around again.

Adley shook her head. "It's out of the question. This isn't even my place to sell. It belongs to Grandpa Jed."

"He's not your grandfather," Susan said with a gentle smile, as if correcting and reminding Adley all at the same time. "You have two very nice grandfathers already."

Adley closed her eyes briefly, and Nate took a protective step toward her. She was outnumbered, and after all that she'd been through today, he wasn't sure how much more she wanted to handle.

"It's been a really long day," Nate said, his voice tight and controlled. "We can probably all agree that right now isn't the best time to discuss such a big decision."

"There's no need to discuss this at all," Adley said. "The answer will still be no."

"That's not acceptable." Rick crossed his arms and planted his feet. "I won't take no for an answer."

"Adley said no." Nate lifted his chin, forcing himself to remain calm. The need to protect Adley overpowered whatever childhood fear or control Rick held over him. Nate was a soldier in the Army National Guard. He had faced warfare in Afghanistan—he could surely face Rick Johnson. "If she doesn't want to discuss it, and she doesn't want to sell, then there's nothing left to say."

Rick clenched his jaw and motioned to Susan and Spencer. "I can see when we're not wanted. Let's go." He started to walk to his car but turned again and said to Adley, "Call me when you aren't being bullied by this soldier, and we'll work out the details. Spencer will be happy to let the buyer know that you're thinking about your asking price."

"I'm not—" Adley's words were cut off when her father got into his car and slammed the door.

Mrs. Johnson looked longingly at her daughter, and then at the house, no doubt wondering about her grandson.

"I'm sorry things happened this way," Spencer said to Adley. "I really would like to discuss the farm a little more with you." He looked at Nate and then back to Adley. "Maybe over supper sometime this week?"

Adley shook her head. "I don't think it's a good idea, Spencer. But thank you for asking."

He offered her a sad smile and nodded. "I understand. Goodbye."

"Bye."

Spencer closed Susan's door and then got into the Porsche. Rick sped off down the drive, kicking up the gravel, before pulling onto the country road.

"I need to sit down." Adley walked to the back porch and took a seat on the hanging swing. She put her face into her hands and let out a long sigh.

Nate took the seat next to her, feeling helpless to offer her comfort. "I wish I could have done something."

"You did." She looked up at him. Even though the sun was completely set now, there was still enough light in the sky for him to see her clearly. "No one has the courage to talk to my dad that way, and I'm happy you did. Unfortunately, he sometimes acts like a three-year-old when he doesn't get what he wants. I appreciate that I had you on my side. It would have been hard to be three against one."

"Any time." And he meant it.

He liked being on Adley's side.

# Chapter Seven

Adley watched as the semitruck pulled out of the driveway. She waved at the driver with a copy of the packing invoice, and he waved back. Inside his truck were the fifty-five-gallon drums full of honey that had been sold to a large company in Iowa that processed and distributed it around the world. The Wilson Honey Company was one of dozens that sold to this particular distributor. It was among their biggest customers, and Adley was so thankful this load was off. The check she would receive from them in a week or two made up a huge percentage of her income. In a few weeks, another shipment would be sent once they were able to extract more of their honey, and then the harvest would be done.

Earlier that morning, Steve and Paul had

gone out to retrieve more of their supers. As August now pushed on to September, they were coming to the end of their extraction season. There were only a few more hives to retrieve, and then Adley would have them shipped off to California for the winter to pollinate the almond groves.

Unfortunately, most of the money she'd already earned through the harvest had been applied to her debt, and daily, she wondered what they would live on through the winter. Her need for the Minnesota Association of Beekeepers grant was greater than ever before. The convention was only four weeks away, and though they had been making steady improvements for the inspection, they still had a lot of work to do. They hadn't even started to tackle the barn, and Adley hadn't found time to talk to Grandpa Jed about the changes she wanted to make.

With Benny napping, Adley used the opportunity to go into the processing room to see the progress with the supers Steve and Paul had brought in that morning.

It was loud and crowded. Grandpa Jed was there, scraping the supers with Paul, while Nate brought in new hives and Steve stacked the empty ones along the wall.

She was met with their smiles, but Nate was the only one who stopped to talk to her.

"I finally had a chance to work on the new packaging labels," he said, above the noise, though she doubted Grandpa Jed or the other two could hear him. "I have it on my laptop in the house. Can I show it to you this evening?"

Adley nodded and then glanced at Grandpa. Would he be okay with her plans to change the look? With Benjamin gone, and her not being a blood relation, it felt strange to make such big decisions. Grandpa was technically retired—yet Adley didn't feel qualified to be calling the shots.

"Steve grabbed the mail when he was coming back in today," Nate said, lifting one of the supers off a stack. His muscles rippled beneath his short sleeves. He was in the best shape of his life, and she couldn't help but notice. He'd always been athletic and strong, but he'd never been quite so masculine. "It's over on the counter. I was going to bring it in at lunch."

"Thanks." She left his side, happy to have an excuse to move away from him.

He'd been at the farm for two weeks now, and it was getting harder and harder for her to look past him. No matter where she turned, he was there, fixing a leaking pipe, replacing a broken window or weed-whipping the overgrown grass along the buildings. He stayed busy—but always within sight. It had been distracting, to say the least. Though not unpleasant. On the contrary, she'd quickly gotten used to having him there. Before he'd come, things had felt quiet—empty. Benjamin's death had left a gaping hole in their lives, even though he'd been deployed for seven months before he died. Nate didn't replace him, but he filled that space that Benjamin had left behind.

Grandpa Jed was happier, Benny loved the extra attention and Adley enjoyed their renewed friendship. It wasn't like it had been in middle school and high school, for obvious reasons. But all of the things she had loved about Nate Marshall hadn't changed—and he had matured and grown in ways that surprised and delighted her.

Adley lifted the stack of mail off the counter and flipped through the envelopes. Her anxiety rose as she saw bill after bill.

But it was the letter with the Minnesota Association of Beekeepers' return address that made her pause. She set down all the others and opened the thin envelope.

Were they writing to tell her that they had changed their minds and she wasn't a finalist anymore? Had she done something wrong to null and void her application?

Slowly, she pulled the letter out and began to read. It didn't take long for her pulse to pick up speed and her mouth to fall open.

Nate must have been watching her, because he came to her side and said, "Bad news?"

She couldn't talk to him about the letter in the processing room where the others might hear, so she motioned for him to step outside.

He didn't question her as they slipped out the back door.

The noise from inside was muted now. Sunshine streamed down upon Adley's shoulders as she looked at the letter again.

"What's wrong?" he finally asked.

"It's a letter from the Minnesota Association of Beekeepers. I don't know why they didn't email, but they're asking us to host the Honeybee Ball in our barn. It will be held the final evening of the convention, and they will announce the winner at the event."

"Doesn't that seem cruel?" Nate asked. "What if you don't win, yet everyone's standing in your barn? Isn't that awkward?"

She shrugged. "I guess it can be. Usually the ball is held in a hotel or convention center, but they said they'd like to start holding it in participating honeybee farm barns. We just happen to be the closest farm to the hosting city. The convention is being held in Timber Falls for the first time this year. If it was being held somewhere else, we wouldn't have to worry about it."

Nate put his hands on his hips as he studied her. "They want to host it in your barn?"

Adley bit her thumbnail. "Yeah."

"Wow. It's one thing to get it cleaned out by inspection day, but it's another thing to get it ready for a party."

"I know." She folded the letter, feeling the disappointment sitting heavy on her heart. "I suppose it's a silly thing to consider. It's just that I'd really like to impress the association so they give us this grant. If I say no, I can't imagine it will make our application look good."

"I didn't say that we shouldn't consider their request." He squinted as he looked deep in thought. "The inspection is in two weeks, but the actual ball is in four weeks, right?"

Adley nodded, pressing her lips together as she watched him.

"That means we have a couple weeks to empty the barn and make the necessary repairs to pass inspection and then a couple more weeks to spruce it up for the ball."

A gentle breeze blew up from Lake Providence as Adley waited. If Nate hadn't been here, there was no way she could even consider such a thing. But he was here, and he was willing to help. Hope mingled with her anxiety. They had to at least try—didn't they?

"We're going to need to talk to Grandpa Jed, Adley." He studied her closely. "About the barn, the new packaging—everything. If we're going to pull this off, everyone needs to be on board. Do you think you can do that?"

She had been putting it off much longer than she should have. And she had a feeling that if she didn't agree to Nate's request, he wouldn't agree to help her. No matter how hard it might be, or how much it might upset Grandpa, she needed to tell him.

"I will." She nodded. "Tonight."

"Good. Because we're going to need to sell all those things in the barn. There's no way we could host a dance in there unless it's gone. We can save some of it—the things that are most important to Grandpa—but the majority of it needs to go."

"Okay." She bit her bottom lip. "I'll do whatever it takes."

"Good. We're going to need to be super focused if we're going to pull this off."

She loved the way he kept using the term "we." It felt good to be a team, and it made her smile, despite her anxiety and uncertainty.

"What?" he asked, matching her smile with his.

Would he really like to know her thoughts? What would he think if she admitted she liked having him there? Maybe it was exactly what she needed to say, to make him realize how much she appreciated him.

"It's nothing. I just like how you keep saying 'we,' as if we're a team."

"We are a team." He reached out and pushed aside a piece of hair that had fallen out of her ponytail and dangled in front of her eye.

She put her hand over his. "Thank you. I truly don't know what I would do without you. I could never even consider doing any of these things if you hadn't come."

His brown eyes were so soft and gentle— so full of affection—it made her heart pump a little harder. He told her that he loved her four years ago, but she had assumed he stopped at some point. Standing here with him now, see-ing how he looked at her, she was suddenly afraid that his feelings hadn't changed.

Was that why he had come back? Now that Benjamin was out of the picture? Was he here to tell her he was still in love with her? She hadn't even considered it, but thinking about it now made her panic increase. Nate couldn't still love her—because if he did, she would have to examine her own heart and figure out her feelings for him once and for all.

If they both loved each other, it would complete their betrayal to Benjamin.

Taking a step back, Adley licked her dry lips and looked away from Nate toward the lake, but it only reminded her of the last time she'd been at the beach—with Nate. She couldn't take the risk that he still cared for her that way. Just thinking about it made her guilt and shame amplify. Benjamin would be so angry if he knew that she was feeling a stir in her heart where Nate was concerned. He'd always thought she loved Nate. She couldn't let Benjamin's accusations become true.

"I'll talk to Grandpa Jed tonight," she said again. "Over supper. Hopefully he'll understand, but if not, I'll have to make him understand. I should get into the kitchen and make something for lunch. Everyone's working so hard. I'm sure they're hungry. Maybe I'll make some soup—or a big salad. I have cookies left over from yesterday's baking." She was rambling, but she couldn't stop. "Can you tell the guys to come in to eat in about thirty minutes?"

Adley didn't even wait for Nate to respond. She turned and walked around the barn to the house, not looking back, afraid she'd see confusion or hurt in Nate's eyes. She owed him so much for all his help—but she couldn't risk giving him her heart.

It had already been given away, and it would be impossible for her to take it back from Benjamin.

Adley's behavior puzzled Nate for the rest of the day. When he went in for lunch, she hadn't met his gaze. When she came out in the afternoon to help in the processing room, she had only spoken to him when necessary. Had he done or said something wrong? He had racked his brain all afternoon to try to remember exactly what he had said to her outside the processing room before she started acting nervous and left him so suddenly—but all he had said was that they were a team.

Had that upset her?

Or maybe was she just nervous about talking to Grandpa Jed? She'd put it off for so long, perhaps she had built it up in her mind bigger than it needed to be.

He had washed up in the processing room before heading toward the house. Now, fresh and clean, he was eager to return to the kitchen. The evenings were his favorite time of the day, when they ate together and then sat on the front porch with Benny until it was time for him to go to bed. The little guy was amazing—and growing so fast. In the two weeks Nate had been there, Benny had already changed.

Nate pulled open the screen door and entered the kitchen. It smelled like roasted chicken and something sweet that he couldn't quite put his finger on. Adley was a great cook, and she seemed to do it so effortlessly. It was a side of her Nate wasn't familiar with, and one that seemed to thrive since she'd become a farmwife.

The moment he entered the house, Benny began to jump in his bouncy chair. His eyes shone bright, and he lifted his hands for Nate to pick him up. Nate happily obliged.

"Hello, buddy." Benny smelled like baby lotion and green beans, and he felt solid in Nate's arms.

Adley turned from the stove and glanced at Nate, and then she looked back at the kettle she was stirring without giving him her customary smile.

Grandpa Jed wasn't in the kitchen, leaving them alone for a minute. Nate wondered if he should ask Adley why she was upset. Would she actually tell him if she was angry at him?

"Ready to talk to Grandpa tonight?" he asked instead, hoping to find a neutral topic to get her to talk.

She was busy mashing potatoes, but she glanced at him quickly and nodded.

"Want to see the packaging design I created?" He started to walk toward the sunroom, but her voice stopped him.

"Maybe later. I think we should start with the barn first. We can talk about repackaging if it comes up. We'll have enough to deal with just focusing on cleaning out the barn for now."

Nate had worked late into the night, several evenings in a row, to get the packaging just right. He was eager to show it to her. "There's no time like the present. Why not tell Grandpa everything and get it over with?"

"Tell me what?" Grandpa Jed asked as he entered the kitchen from the direction of his bedroom, sliding a comb through his thin hair.

Adley returned to her mashed potatoes. "Let's wait until supper is served before we talk."

Grandpa looked between Adley and Nate, one of his eyebrows raised in question.

"Here," Nate said to Grandpa. "Can you hold

Benny while I help Adley get the rest of the meal on the table?"

"I can manage without you," Adley said, her voice a little tighter than he'd heard it before.

He paused, and so did Grandpa. Neither of them moved for a moment, and then Nate handed the baby to Grandpa Jed and went to Adley.

"Is everything okay?" he asked, quietly. Had he pushed her too far with asking her to talk to Grandpa Jed about all the changes she needed to make before she was ready?

"It's fine." She scooped the mashed potatoes into a serving bowl, her movements a little awkward.

"It doesn't seem fine. You've been avoiding me all afternoon. Did I do something to upset you?"

She motioned for him to move away from the oven and used some hot pads to remove the chicken. After she set the roasting pan on the counter, she turned off the burners on the stove and dished up the gravy and steamed green beans that Nate had just picked in the garden that morning.

"Adley?" he asked, frowning. "Are you mad at me?"

"I'm not mad at you, Nate, just—" She paused and set her hands on the countertop, her face softening a fraction. "I'm overwhelmed right now. Okay? I need a little space."

She needed space? What kind of space? Had he been crowding her?

Slowly, he took the mashed potatoes and put them on the table and then went back to start carving the chicken.

Grandpa Jed was quiet as he watched them.

Nate didn't know if he should feel embarrassed, apologetic or angry. He'd been trying hard to keep Adley at a respectable distance, knowing she was still grieving Benjamin's death, dealing with the responsibilities of the farm and adjusting to having him there. He had tried to be helpful without being in her way. Was he the one overwhelming her? Or just life in general? She hadn't treated Grandpa, Steve or Paul the way she'd treated him.

He was determined to talk to her about whatever was bothering her, but now wasn't that time.

Within minutes, they had supper on the table. Nate put Benny in his high chair as Adley finally came to sit down.

After Grandpa Jed prayed, they dug into the meal.

The chicken was moist, the mashed potatoes were creamy and the green beans were crisp. It was a delicious meal, but no one was complimenting Adley tonight. They didn't say a word.

It was the most uncomfortable Nate had been since he'd arrived.

"So," Grandpa Jed finally said. "What's wrong?"

He spoke to both of them, but his gaze landed on Adley and stayed there.

Adley moved her potatoes around her plate as she looked down at her food. When she glanced up, she met Grandpa Jed's gaze and said, "I haven't wanted to tell you, but we're struggling with our finances."

"Yeah?" Grandpa Jed nodded, thoughtful. "I can't remember a time when we didn't struggle with our finances on this farm. It's not an easy life, always living from one year to the next, hoping and praying God meets all our needs, trusting Him when He chooses not to. It's the way farmers live."

"It's more than that." Adley set down her fork and folded her hands. "If something doesn't change soon, I don't think we'll make it through the winter."

Nate watched Grandpa Jed closely, seeing if this alarmed him. It was hard to read his thoughts behind his steady gaze. Either nothing fazed him, or he had learned how to control his emotions years ago.

"I have applied for a grant through the Minnesota Association of Beekeepers," Adley continued. "We're one of the finalists, but the association will need to inspect our farm, and they've asked us to host a ball in the barn during the convention."

"Oh." That got Grandpa Jed's attention. "*Our* barn?"

"Yes." Adley swallowed hard. "And I don't feel like we can refuse their request without it hurting our prospects for the grant."

"Have you seen the barn?" Grandpa Jed asked. "We can't host a ball there."

"We could," Nate spoke up, belatedly realizing that he might be overstepping his boundaries. Was that why Adley was upset? He had kept saying "we" while they made plans, but this clearly wasn't his farm. Had that upset her?

"What are you thinking?" Grandpa Jed asked him.

Nate glanced at Adley and instead of looking upset, she looked relieved that he was chiming in. The look encouraged him to continue. "I've glanced at some of the things in the barn, and I believe that a lot of it is really valuable to collectors. It would take us a couple of weeks, but I think we could get it sorted. We'll need some dumpsters, because not all of it is worth something. And we'll need to bring in an antiques appraiser to see what we've—you've got out there. But I think it would be really beneficial. We can clean out the barn for the ball and raise some much-needed funds."

"Hmm." Grandpa Jed rubbed his chin as he looked down at his plate. "That stuff's been collecting there for as long as I can remember. When my great-grandfather switched the farm from dairy to bees, it just became a storage space. I never touched it, because, frankly, I didn't have the time or interest in figuring out what was all in there." He looked up at Nate. "Would you be willing to oversee the project? It would be a big one."

Nate glanced at Adley again, trying to gauge whether or not she wanted him to be in charge. Her simple nod was all he needed. "I'd be happy to help."

"Well, now." Grandpa dipped his fork into his mashed potatoes. "I didn't think I'd see it done in my lifetime, but I'm kind of excited to get it cleaned out. I even know an appraiser who I could call and see if he'd come take a look at some of it."

"Really?" Adley asked. "You're not upset?"

"Upset?" Grandpa chuckled. "Upset that the farm is struggling and we'll need to be creative to figure out how to make ends meet? Sounds pretty familiar."

"I thought you'd be angry or disappointed in me."

"Angry?" Grandpa reached out and took her hand in his. "How could I be angry that you're fighting for our farm? Until Benjamin and you took over, I thought I'd have to sell. Then when Benjamin died, I thought surely you'd want to move on. Knowing that you want to take care of this farm makes me happier than I've been in years. The thought that little Benny will have this legacy to carry on if he so chooses gives me a sense of satisfaction I've never known before."

Tears sprang to Adley's eyes, and she put her free hand over Grandpa Jed's.

Nate felt like an intruder in this moment. This was their home, their farm, their hopes and dreams. He didn't belong here. He knew it and Adley knew it.

As he'd been helping these past two weeks, remembering all the times he'd worked on the farm in high school, he had felt a sense of belonging and ownership, but this conversation was a stark reminder that he had no investment here. He was only helping for a short season, and then he'd have to move on.

No wonder Adley had been feeling like she needed space.

"There's something else," Adley said. "We have a new honey competitor in town."

Grandpa nodded. "I saw. Sweet Basil Honey. They have some eye-catching packaging."

Adley looked excited as she sat up straighter in her chair. "Nate has some ideas about how we can change our packaging. He's been working on a new logo and wants to show it to us."

"Really?" Grandpa Jed turned to study Nate. "I didn't know you could do that."

Nate smiled and nodded. "I'd be happy to show it to you after we're done with supper."

"I'd love to see it." Grandpa Jed returned his smile. "If we're going to find a way to save this farm, we need to be willing to compromise and innovate, right?"

"Right." Nate glanced at Adley.

There was a light in her eyes that hadn't been there before, and for the first time since he'd arrived, he could see a weight lifted off her shoulders.

When she met his gaze, though, that same reservation returned. Something was off, and he was determined to figure out what had her upset.

# Chapter Eight

After the talk with Grandpa, Adley wasn't quite sure why she'd been so nervous to have the conversation with him. It had gone better than she anticipated, and he had taken all the changes in stride. Was she the one afraid of the changes all along? Or was she just afraid to move on now that Benjamin was gone? Keeping things the way he had left them felt like she had been holding on to him in some way, but it wasn't healthy for her or the farm.

She closed the washing machine lid and pressed Start, hiding a yawn behind her hand as she left the laundry room and entered the kitchen. Both Benny and Grandpa were in bed, and Nate had disappeared somewhere once he had shown his designs to her and Grandpa after supper. All of his options had impressed her, but it was easy to pick out the one she liked best. The label was yellow and wrapped around the jar, but the sides were cut out in the shape of honeybee wings and extended beyond the jar, so it looked like the jar could take flight. Adley had been concerned that it would be expensive, but Nate had already found a company that could mass-produce the labels for a fraction of the cost she had assumed. The new design would be eye-catching and hopefully increase sales.

With Grandpa's approval, they had placed their first order and should have the labels within the week.

Along with the new labels, he had created a website with the same branding and shared pictures he had taken on the farm while they worked the past two weeks. It made the website—and farm—feel personal and trustworthy. Another bonus for marketing to new customers. There was a link for people to purchase the honey directly from Adley. Nate explained how everything worked and launched the website as they sat at the dining room table. Adley had never even contemplated a website. They'd done business the old-fashioned way ever since she and Benjamin had taken over. But with the additional income they could bring in from the website, she felt another boost of optimism.

The house was quiet as the sun set on the horizon. Adley wanted to thank Nate, again, and apologize for the way she had treated him earlier. She had resolved to think the best of him, especially since he had given her no reason to believe his intentions were less than honorable. Fear had prompted her behavior, and she wouldn't let it continue.

He wasn't on the front porch or in the sunroom. When she stepped onto the back porch, she saw the large barn doors open, revealing the treasures within.

Sommer ran up to Adley and followed close on her heels as she crossed the barnyard. She reached down and petted Sommer's silky head and then threw the tennis ball for her just before she entered the barn.

"Nate?" Adley asked. "Are you in here?"

"Yeah. I'm back here." He spoke from a corner of the barn.

It was hard to pinpoint exactly where he was with all the junk. But Adley moved toward his voice. "I feel like I might need to play Marco Polo to find you."

Nate chuckled and moved away from a stack of wood crates. The setting sun, coming through the open barn doors, made his brown eyes sparkle. His smile was so sincere, and so handsome, it sent an unexpected warmth through her midsection.

"I did have a brief moment of panic that I would get buried alive in here and no one would be able to find me." He had a rusted, heavy-looking chain in his hands. "I think this might be an old logging chain. I remember seeing something like it at the county historical society when I was a kid." He set it in a crate and wiped his hands on his jeans. It left a mark, but he didn't seem to mind. "There's no telling what we'll find in here. It's kind of exciting."

The barn was dusty and smelled like old, rotting wood, mildew and forgotten dreams. Adley noticed an old steamer trunk, a dress form, an antique motorcycle and tons of other items that had a story to tell.

"Isn't it amazing to think that all of this stuff was purchased, probably with the money made on this farm—and for what?" Adley touched a stack of vintage *Time* magazines. "Why do we work so hard to acquire so much stuff and then shove it away for someone else to deal with later? It kind of feels like a waste. This barn really puts life in perspective, doesn't it?"

Nate touched the old weather vane, and it creaked as the blades turned. "It's a good reminder to store up for ourselves treasures in heaven where moth and rust don't destroy, isn't it? Makes me wonder if Jesus had a barn like this in mind when He shared that piece of scripture."

Adley smiled to herself, remembering sitting next to Nate during Sunday school and youth group. He'd always been a curious student who had asked dozens of questions each week. Their Sunday school teacher, Mrs. Brown, had been impatient with him, but the youth group pastor had loved him.

Adley and Grandpa hadn't been able to go to church last Sunday, since Benny had been running a fever, but she hoped to go tomorrow. Nate had said he wanted to go, too.

"I had a thought," Nate said as he walked around the crates and came to stand next to Adley. "As we go through all of this, it would be fun to keep some of the more unique items, or the ones special to this farm, and use it to decorate the barn for the ball. I saw some old Wilson Honey Farm signs along the back wall. It would be cool to hang them up for everyone to see."

"I love that idea."

"When it's all decorated and cleaned up, you should consider renting the space out for small weddings and events. It could be a source of income."

Adley smiled. "Another great idea." She studied him in the dying light. "You've been a big help, Nate. In two short weeks, I have several new possible streams of income, and you're the guy to thank."

He shrugged. "It's easy to brainstorm ideas when I don't have any skin in the game. I have a feeling that if I was the one in charge, with so much riding on my shoulders, I probably wouldn't be able to see things so objectively. It isn't hard to offer suggestions when I'm not the one taking any risks."

"I wouldn't say that you don't have any skin in the game. You're here, investing in our future, when you could be anywhere else."

Nate put his hand on a stack of old chairs and shrugged again. "I'm just fulfilling a promise to Benjamin."

"It's more than that. You've been encouraging, helpful and fun to be around. You've—you've been like the old Nate. The one I remember."

"I never changed, Adley."

His serious comment stopped her train of thought, and she studied him. "Yeah, but—after what you said to me before the wedding—things changed—didn't they?" She frowned, wondering why she was bringing this up now, of all times. She had come out here to apologize for how she had behaved earlier—not talk about the past. Yet weren't the two connected?

He was quiet for a moment, a dozen different emotions playing in his gaze. She wished she knew what he was thinking, but then again, did she want to know?

"Things changed," he agreed, "but maybe not in the way you think. I always knew I had been in love with you. The only thing that changed was that you knew, too."

She swallowed at the revelation. Nothing else had changed—yet it had felt like everything had changed. One complicated conversation and her entire world had been different. Not only had she lost one of her best friends, but she had started to second-guess how she felt about him, too.

"I'm the same man I was before you knew," Nate said gently.

"Four years has changed both of us."

"True. But the most important things are the same." He frowned. "Why were you upset at me earlier? And don't say you weren't. You wear your emotions on your sleeve. I could always tell when I had upset you—the only difference is that I usually knew how I had done it. This time, I'm clueless."

Did she want him to know her fears? It would

be awkward to tell him that she was afraid he was still in love with her.

"I'm sorry about that." She ran the toe of her flip-flops across the dirt floor of the barn. "I'm just trying to work through some things."

"Did I do something to upset you?"

"No—and I'm being honest. You haven't done a thing to make me upset." She chuckled to herself. "At least, not recently. You've upset me plenty in the past."

He smiled. "Good. I want to keep open communication between us at all times. I think that's where things went wrong when we were younger. If I had been open and honest with you from the start, maybe things would have been different."

"Maybe." Her word felt small and insignificant, because if things had been different, then she wouldn't be here on the farm, raising Benny and taking care of Grandpa Jed. As hard as those jobs were, she wouldn't change them for the world. "Or maybe things turned out exactly how they were supposed to."

A sad smile tilted up Nate's lips. "Maybe." He paused for a moment. "Just promise me that you'll tell me what's on your mind, no matter how hard the conversation might be. I don't want to overstep my boundaries here, and I don't want you to ever feel like you can't talk to me. Okay?"

"Okay. And I want the same from you."

"You got it, boss." He winked.

Adley playfully swatted at him. "I'm going to start calling you by your childhood nickname if you don't stop that—Natertot."

Nate's face immediately became serious. "There's no need to make threats."

Laughing, Adley shook her head. "It's getting late, and we have to be up early for church in the morning. I think I'll head in."

"I'll come with you."

They closed the barn doors together, and Nate picked up Sommer's ball to throw for her again. The sun had disappeared, and a few stars had become visible in the night sky.

Adley felt peaceful for the first time in a long time. Hope had found a place in her heart and had nuzzled in, making itself at home. With Nate at her side, she felt like anything was possible again.

She hadn't felt that way in years.

Timber Falls Community Church looked a lot different than it used to when Nate was a kid. A large school had been added on to the back of the church where a house used to stand.

Nate stood in the parking lot for a minute, admiring the progress—and stalling his entrance into the church.

"Everything okay?" Adley asked as she unlatched Benny's car seat from the back of the double-cab truck. Insurance had paid for the dents from the hail, and Nate had just picked it up from the auto body shop yesterday. It looked as good as new.

"Yeah." He hated to admit to her that he was nervous to be back at church. It was one thing to pop in and out of businesses in town where people might know him, but no one *really* knew him. Church was different. He and his mom had attended Timber Falls Community Church ever since he and Adley had become friends. Everyone had known his dad had abandoned them, they all knew when his mom had taken on a third job just to make ends meet, and they had been there to watch Nate make a lot of dumb decisions through middle school. Granted, the church had rallied around him and his mom when they were in need—but not everyone had been kind to him.

People like Rick Johnson had been judgmental and had looked down their noses at Nate and his mom. For some reason, he wasn't thinking about the kind and loving people who would welcome him back with open arms. All he could think about were the Rick Johnsons of the church who would be judging his life choices and finding him lacking.

And what would they think when they saw him come in with Adley? As a young widow, would they think he was trying to date her? Would they think it was wrong, since Benjamin had been his best friend? Would they think his intentions were honorable?

Worse, would they think he wasn't good enough for her?

Adley tossed a curious smile at him and then walked toward the back door. Grandpa Jed moved along beside her at a slow pace since his arthritis had been acting up that morning, but he was determined to come to church.

Nate jogged ahead of them and opened the door for Adley and Grandpa to walk into the building.

Cool air rippled across his skin as he followed them in. The back hallway ran the length of this side of the church. Coat hooks lined the wall, though they weren't used much during the hot summer months.

"I'm going to take Benny to the nursery," Adley said to the men. "I'll meet you in the sanctuary."

Nate wanted to offer to go with her, but he wasn't sure if she'd think that was weird. At some point, he'd have to face the church family—and one person in particular.

His mom.

She didn't even know he was in Timber Falls. He had a feeling she'd be upset when she found out he'd been in town for two weeks and hadn't stopped by. But he hadn't been able to bring himself to initiate the reunion. His mom was an amazing woman and had sacrificed so much for him—yet she was hard to please, and he often felt like he wasn't enough. She always seemed disappointed in him, no matter what he did. It had become easier just to ignore her and put some space between them.

"I'm going to use the men's room," Grandpa Jed said. "I'll meet you and Adley in the sanctuary."

Nate opened his mouth to protest being alone to face his mom but realized how ridiculous it would sound to Grandpa Jed if he did. Instead, he stood for a few seconds in the back hall by himself, trying to get up the nerve to enter the fellowship hall where he could hear a cacophony of voices.

Maybe his mom wouldn't be at church today.

With that thought in mind, he took a deep breath and followed the noise.

At first, he just stood in the fellowship hall, studying the faces of the congregants. Most of them were unfamiliar to him—more than he anticipated. There were a lot of younger people there, families with little kids. A few were older individuals who either had changed so much in four years that he didn't recognize them or were new. Slowly, he started to identify a few people he remembered—and they started to notice him.

One of the ladies, Mrs. Evans, broke away from the gaggle of church ladies she was with and said, "Nate Marshall! Or should I call you Lieutenant Marshall? How are you?"

"Nate's just fine." He smiled and then watched as several of the other ladies joined them. Mrs. Caruthers, Mrs. Anderson and Mrs. Topper all gathered around him, throwing questions at him faster than he could answer.

"What are you doing home?"

"Does your mother know you're here? She hasn't said anything."

"Are you married? Have a special gal?"

"Where are you living?"

"What are you doing for a living now?"

"How was Afghanistan? Isn't it horrible

about what happened to Benjamin? We heard you were there when it happened. Have you seen Adley? Isn't it a shame that she's a widow at such a young age?"

"She's not the only young widow this church has seen," Mrs. Evans said. "Piper was a widow at twenty-seven. But then again, we took care of that problem, didn't we?"

The ladies giggled, and Nate felt like he was drowning under all their chatter. He wanted to come up for air, but Mrs. Evans continued.

"You heard Piper Pierson married Nick Connelly? Right? And then Nick died in a construction accident and Piper married my son, Max Evans. You heard that Max was playing for the NFL, right? Well, he retired and came back to coach my younger son, Tad. He took the high school football team to State and won. They've actually won two years in a row now, thanks to Max."

Nate's mouth slipped open as he tried to absorb all the information she was tossing at him.

"We've had a lot of weddings here lately," Mrs. Anderson added. "Joy Gordon married Chase Asher, and they have a whole passel of kids. Then our very own pastor, Jacob Dawson, married Kate LeClair—"

"She was a professional actress on Broadway," Mrs. Caruthers added as she watched Nate's reaction. "But her cousin died and left the triplets and the house to Kate, so she came to Timber Falls and gave it all up for them. They also have the pastor's daughter, Maggie, and a little girl, Caroline, together now. Five children in all—and I wouldn't be surprised if they had another soon."

"And then there was Liv Butler," Mrs. Anderson continued. "She married Zane Harris and they're expecting a child this winter."

"Don't forget about Knox Taylor," Mrs. Evans said. "He married Merritt Lane."

"Does that count, though?" Mrs. Anderson asked. "They got married out at the lake."

"Right," Mrs. Evans agreed. "But they still come to church here. So, yes, it counts."

Nate would never remember all these names—and he was surprised to realize he felt relieved when he saw his mom enter through the front doors of the church.

"Ladies," he said, "my mom just arrived. It was nice to visit with you, but I should go over and talk to her."

"Of course," Mrs. Evans said. "We'll catch up later."

He smiled, hoping he didn't have to endure another avalanche of information from them, as he moved away from the ladies and met his mom near the front of the fellowship hall. When she glanced at him, she didn't appear to recognize him at first—and then she did and her eyes grew wide.

"Nate! What are you doing here?"

"Hi, Mom." He leaned in and placed a kiss on her cheek. "Surprise."

"Surprise is right." She looked him over, taking his arm to turn him around so she could see all sides of him. Her dark hair was sprinkled with gray and her brown eyes had more wrinkles at the corners, but other than that, she looked exactly like she did when he was in high school. "You look healthy."

"I feel healthy."

"I haven't heard from you since your welcome-home event in Saint Paul. I was wondering when you might come north to see me."

Adley appeared on the other side of the fellowship hall. Though his mom had always liked her, she had agreed with Rick Johnson and often told Nate that Adley was out of his reach, that he should pursue someone more in his league. He hadn't talked to his mom about Adley very much, but she would have been blind not to notice Nate's feelings for her in high school.

Even now, Mom's gaze followed his, and she crossed her arms, her mouth turning down in displeasure. "I hope you're not back in town because she's single again. I think you would have learned your lesson the hard way."

"Ouch."

"Well?" She raised her eyebrows at him.

He let out a sigh. "Benjamin asked me to come back and help her out. It was his last request."

"Oh." Mom lowered her arms. "I'm sorry, Nate. That must have been hard."

"Yeah." He saw that Adley was walking toward them and knew he needed to explain fast. "I've been staying at the Wilson farm for a couple of weeks, working on the harvest. Adley and Grandpa Jed need the help."

Mom raised her eyebrows again, but this time she looked hurt. "And you didn't call or stop by?"

"I've been really busy."

"Too busy to pick up your phone and give me a quick call or text to let me know you've been less than fifteen miles away? I haven't seen you since you came back from Afghanistan. It would have been nice to set eyes on you before now."

"Sorry," he said again.

Adley finally joined them, a smile on her pretty face. "Hello, Mrs. Marshall."

"Hi, Adley." Mom offered Adley a tight smile. "Nate tells me he's been staying at your farm."

Adley turned her appreciative gaze to Nate and nodded. There was something warm and sweet in her face—and it tightened Nate's chest with pleasure. It had been a long time since she'd looked at him that way. And he liked it—a lot. In that moment, he was pretty sure he'd do just about anything to have her keep looking at him like that.

"I don't know what I'd do without him," Adley said. "He's been a lifesaver."

"Well." Mom looked from Adley to Nate, and back to Adley. "I'd be careful. You two wouldn't want people to get the wrong idea about you."

Adley's smile fell, and Nate's pleasure disappeared.

The sanctuary doors opened, and people started to enter for the service. Music was pouring through the doors, calling people in to worship.

"It was nice to see you again," Mom said to Adley, and then looked to Nate. "It wouldn't hurt for you to stop by some time and say hi.

Let me know when you have a minute or two. That's all I'm asking for."

Nate nodded, still a little stunned from her last statement. He looked around the sanctuary and noticed a few people looking in his direction—and then he spotted Rick and Susan Johnson as they entered with Spencer Ford. The trio stood out in their expensive suits, reminding the world that they were wealthy and powerful.

And Nate realized what his mom meant. He wasn't good enough for Adley, and everyone knew it. He wouldn't want people to get the wrong idea that he was setting his sights too high.

He'd been right all along. Not much changed in Timber Falls.

# Chapter Nine

As the service ended, Adley still couldn't shake Mrs. Marshall's comment from her mind. Nate walked beside her as they left the sanctuary, and she found herself looking around to see if people were watching them. *Would* they get the wrong idea about her and Nate? And if they did, what kind of idea would they get? She'd been a widow for over six months. It wasn't a long time, but was it wrong for her to be seen with a single man already? Was that the wrong idea people were getting? That it was too soon for her to move on?

She wanted to tell Mrs. Marshall that she wasn't moving on—not with Nate. Adley wasn't even sure she'd ever move on again. Marriage was hard, and she hadn't been any good at it the first time.

"Hello, Nate." An older woman, Mrs. Brown, approached him and nodded briefly at Adley before turning her attention back to Nate. She'd been a fixture at Timber Falls Community Church as long as Adley could remember, teaching various Sunday school classes, volunteering on the women's ministry board and generally poking her nose into other people's business. She hadn't been patient with Nate when they were in middle school. "I hope the military has cleaned up your act a bit."

Nate's back went rigid, but he didn't respond.

Adley stared at the woman, surprised at the tone of her voice and the accusation in her words. She wasn't laughing or teasing. Sadly, given Mrs. Brown's history, her comment shouldn't have surprised Adley. It was unfortunate that she was a representative of their church, though there were so many other kind and thoughtful people who made up for Mrs. Brown's lack of warmth.

"I always told your mother that a boy needs a father," Mrs. Brown continued. "I warned her that you'd grow up to be a nuisance if something wasn't done about it—and for a time there, you were. Sometimes the military can step in and be the father figure a man needs. I hope you learned your lessons well."

Nate glanced at Adley, and she tried to mask the shock she felt at this woman's harsh words. Memories from Sunday school resurfaced. Mrs. Brown had always seemed harsh and judgmental of Nate even back then. Adley had always known Nate had suffered from the stigma that came after his dad left—but she hadn't realized, until this moment, how hard it must have been for him to endure—all because of a choice his dad had made.

"I always thought Nate was a wonderful kid," Adley said, offering him a smile while speaking to Mrs. Brown. "He's turned into an even better man. Hardship creates character—and Nate has great character. I hope Benny grows up to be just like him."

Both Nate and the older woman looked at Adley.

But it was Nate's smile that captured Adley's heart.

Mrs. Brown's demeanor changed, and she lowered her chin demurely. "I suppose you would be a good judge of character, Adley, having been raised by such upstanding parents. Your dad was an elder here at church for most of your life. You couldn't help but be a good kid." She looked back at Nate, the disdain returning. "I suppose I should trust Adley's opinion of you, though it goes against everything I've always known to be true. I suppose your mother did the best she could."

Nate pressed his lips together for a second and then said, "My mother did better than you can imagine, and to be honest, I think it was best that my dad left. I would probably be a lot more scarred if he had stayed."

The woman's mouth dropped open, and without another word, she turned away from them.

After she left, Adley leaned into Nate as they continued out of the sanctuary. "I never realized how difficult it must have been for you growing up without your dad. I'm so sorry she treated you that way."

"It couldn't have been easy for you to live up to people's expectations, especially because of your dad."

"It's sad that people assume the best and worst of others by outward appearances—or by their parents' decisions." Adley looked up at Nate, wishing she could go back and change things for him. "I shouldn't be judged based on my dad's reputation any more than you should be."

"Speaking of your dad…"

Adley shifted her gaze and saw her parents waiting for them just outside the sanctuary doors. Spencer was with them, chatting with Mrs. Brown. She was smiling sweetly at him, staring up at him like he was astonishing. When Nate and Adley approached, she made her exit and left the building.

"Good morning, Adley," Dad said to her. He nodded in Nate's direction. "Nate."

"Hello, Mr. John—"

"Adley," Dad interrupted Nate and turned his focus back on Adley. "Your mom and I are hoping to take you and Benny out for lunch today. We thought it would be nice to visit the Pine Edge Inn, for old times' sake. They have those orange rolls you always loved so much."

"I drove in with Grandpa and Nate—"

"They won't mind going home without you. Your mother and I can take you out to the farm later, after we've enjoyed time with you and the boy."

"You go on," Grandpa Jed said, coming up behind Adley. He put his hand on her arm. "Nate and I can fend for ourselves for a few hours. It would be good for you to get away with your parents. Benny needs that time with his grandma and grandpa, too."

Dad gave Grandpa Jed a look, as if to say Adley could make up her own mind and didn't need his permission to spend the day with her parents.

She knew she wouldn't get away with turning him down. He'd keep asking her every time he saw her until she said yes. And it would be nice to visit with her mom for a while. They hadn't done much of it since Benny was born, though Mom had come out to the farm a couple of times right after his birth.

"Okay. I'll just get Benny from the nursery, and we'll meet you in the parking lot." Adley turned to Nate. "You don't mind, do you?"

He smiled. "You don't need to ask me for permission."

A part of her had hoped he'd protest. She'd been looking forward to a lazy day with him on the farm. They had both agreed that Sundays were meant for rest, and Adley had hoped they could go down to the lake with Benny to take him swimming.

But if Nate didn't seem to mind that she wouldn't be at the farm, then she really had no other reason to turn down her father.

Ten minutes later, Adley had Benny in his car seat out in the parking lot. She waved goodbye to Nate and Grandpa Jed as they pulled away and then found her parents.

She couldn't deny she was disappointed that she wasn't with Grandpa Jed and Nate.

"We invited Spencer to come with us to lunch," Dad said.

Spencer was there, a smile on his face. "I've been hoping to get more time in your company," he said to Adley, offering to take Benny from her. He held the car seat, with the baby inside, like it weighed next to nothing.

"I told him I was happy to share you." Dad opened the front door of his Porsche for Mom.

It was a tight squeeze in the back with Benny's car seat between Adley and Spencer. Benny quickly fell asleep on the car ride to the hotel restaurant, and Spencer didn't seem to mind how compact they were. He kept smiling at Adley and then looking down at Benny with a tender gaze.

Dad glanced at the three of them in his rearview mirror from time to time, a pleased gleam in his eyes, and Mom looked over her shoulder to wink at Adley.

Adley wanted to groan. Even if her parents were trying to play matchmaker, they could at least be a little more subtle.

Lunch went well, though Benny woke up and demanded to be fed. Thankfully, he was able to sit up in a high chair and loved the little pieces of orange roll Adley gave him.

After lunch, they went to her parents' house, on the banks of the Mississippi River. It was a sprawling home on a perfectly manicured lot. The neighborhood was well-established and one of the nicest in town. Adley couldn't deny that it felt wonderful to sit on the back patio again, watching the gentle water float past, as her mother served iced tea and her famous lemon-ginger cookies.

"You know," Mom said as she took Benny out of Adley's arms and sat with him on a chair across from her, "I would love to have the opportunity to babysit this little guy from time to time. My schedule is always wide-open, and now that he's a little older, it would be so much fun. All you need to do is ask."

Other than Grandpa Jed, Adley had never had a babysitter for Benny. It didn't occur to her to ask her mom, since her dad was usually averse to little kids, and her mother's life revolved around all her volunteer activities. But Dad was sitting there, listening to his wife's offer, and he didn't say no.

"Okay," Adley said slowly. It was a relief to know that if Grandpa Jed wasn't able to physically handle babysitting any longer, her mom was a great option.

"Good." Mom grinned and then started to bounce Benny on her lap, chatting with the little guy as her dad looked on, a pleased expression on his face.

Spencer sat next to Adley, watching the family interact. When she glanced at him, he smiled. "I'd love a family of my own."

The comment surprised her. "Oh?"

"I spent too much time on my education and then my career. I always thought I'd have time to look for someone special to share my life, but this past year, I've started to fear that my opportunities have passed me by."

Adley didn't know what to say, so she said the only thing she could think. "You still have time."

"I'm happy to hear you say that."

She smiled politely, thinking the conversation was done, but Spencer went on.

"I think the best opportunity of my life is sitting next to me right now."

His words rendered her speechless. How was she supposed to respond to that?

"I know I might be coming on strong," Spencer said as he readjusted himself to better face her. Thankfully, he was speaking quietly enough that her parents appeared to not hear them. "I like you, Adley, and I hope I can get to know you better."

Adley started to fidget in her seat, feeling horribly uncomfortable. Was this why her parents were playing matchmaker, because Spencer had told them he liked her? Or was he coming on strong because her parents had told him he needed to get her attention? If that was the case, it had worked.

She looked down at the tea in her hands and bit her upper lip as she considered how to respond. "I'm flattered—really. It's just that I—it's too soon. I'm still trying to get a handle on my new normal. I don't think I'll ever date again."

"That's nonsense," Dad said with a frown.

Both Adley and Spencer looked up at him. At first, Adley thought he was talking to her mom, but then he looked right at Adley, apparently very aware of their conversation. "You're young and you weren't all that happy with Benjamin, so why miss a chance with Spencer? You've made enough mistakes in your life. You don't need to make another one."

"Dad!" Adley set down her iced tea and frowned at him. "It's none of your business, to begin with, but can you have some tact? I'd rather not discuss the failings of my marriage in front of a guest."

"Why not? Spencer knows everything there is to know about you."

"I've even shown him your baby books," Mom said with a gentle smile.

Adley couldn't believe her parents. "I'd like to live my own life, if you don't mind."

"It's okay," Spencer said, looking just as uncomfortable as Adley felt. "I understand. I won't rush you."

"Thank you." She tried to regain a semblance of control.

"If we're not going to talk about you and Spencer dating," Dad said, "then let's talk about that farm of yours. The buyers are extremely interested, and I know we can get top dollar."

"Dad!" Adley said again as she stood. "If you just brought me here to try to manipulate me, then I'm ready to leave."

"Sit down," Dad said. "We don't need to talk about the farm—right now."

"Good." Adley resumed her seat. "I don't want to talk about it again."

No one said anything for a moment, and then Dad started to talk to Spencer about golf. "Did you hear the PGA is hosting a US Open qualifier in Timber Falls next May?"

Adley wanted to sigh in relief but knew this reprieve wouldn't last long.

She couldn't wait to get home where no one pressured her to be someone or something she was not.

Nate was already sweating, and it wasn't even nine in the morning. The enormous dumpster had been delivered around eight, and Nate hadn't wasted any time starting to go through the barn. Grandpa Jed had even bypassed his morning drive into Timber Falls to help, though Nate told him to take it easy and stop often for rests. But Grandpa was having a good day, and he seemed energized to tackle the junk stacked high in the barn.

"I wonder why Adley hasn't shown herself this morning," Grandpa said absently as he looked through a box of random tools.

They had one trailer backed up to the barn to put the items in that they planned to sell, and another trailer beside it, for things they planned to donate to the local charity thrift store. The giveaway pile was starting to grow, but they had only found a few things that they thought might be worth some money to sell. The appraiser would come out at the end of the week to look over everything before they took stuff to the dump.

The dumpster was filling up faster than anything.

Nate tossed an old, rusted chicken feeder into the dumpster and glanced at the house, hoping to see Adley.

"She got in pretty late last night," he said to Grandpa. "I was already in bed when I heard her tiptoe through the kitchen."

"I'm happy she got to spend some time with her parents." Grandpa tossed an old handsaw into the dumpster. "There's a lot of healing that needs to happen there."

A few minutes later, Adley finally came out to the barn. She had Benny in a back carrier and wore her hair in a bun. Her eyes were shining, and she looked refreshed. The baby also appeared happy, his legs dangling down and drool dripping from his bottom lip as he grinned at Nate.

"Good morning," Adley said. "Sorry I didn't get out here sooner. Benny and I slept in, and then he had a blowout in his diaper and needed a bath."

"We're doing okay," Grandpa said. "How was your day with your parents?"

Nate watched Adley's expression as he lifted

an old, broken rocking chair off the pile in the barn. Something shifted in her face, making her look a little less relaxed and a lot more annoyed.

"Other than the fact that my parents are trying to set me up with Spencer Ford, it was a lovely day."

It took a lot of control, but Nate was able to keep his face neutral. He didn't have anything against Spencer—he just didn't like him.

"Spencer?" Grandpa wrinkled his nose in a rare show of judgment. "He might be right for someone, but I don't think he's right for you and Benny."

"Oh?" Adley smiled. "You have an opinion about who is right and wrong for us?"

Grandpa smiled to himself as he lifted a broken hammer out of the box and tossed it into the dumpster. "I sure do."

Nate tried not to appear like he was eavesdropping, though it was impossible.

Grandpa Jed didn't elaborate.

Adley looked at Nate and shook her head, though she was still smiling.

She walked into the barn and looked at the small dent they had made in the past hour. "Wow," was all she said.

"Yeah," Nate agreed. "The more we take out, the more that seems to appear."

They worked side by side for a few minutes. Adley was able to help him haul out some of the bigger items, even with Benny on her back.

"Want me to take him for a while?" Nate asked. "I wouldn't mind wearing the carrier. It would free you up a little more."

Her green eyes lit up with appreciation, but she shook her head. "I don't mind. He'll be ready for his morning nap soon."

Benny pulled at Adley's bun, completely mesmerized by his mother's hair. She made a face, as if he was hurting her, and put her hand back there to stop him. He started to cry.

"Okay, okay," she said. "Play with my hair." As soon as she removed her hands, he stopped crying and began to tug at her bun again.

Nate loved watching Adley with her son. It was still strange to him that she was a mom, but she was as natural as any woman he'd ever seen. And Benny was a funny little guy, full of curiosity. Nate couldn't help but wonder what he would do with his life. Would he want to continue working on the farm, go to college or start his own business? There were so many possibilities, and Nate thought it would be fun to show Benny all the things that life had to offer.

"Well, lookee here," Grandpa said with a chuckle, pulling Nate's thoughts away from Adley and Benny.

Grandpa tapped a wooden crate with his boot. "Some old beekeeping tools and paraphernalia. Looks like they're some of the originals."

Nate and Adley went over to look at what Grandpa had found. Even Benny seemed interested as he stopped playing with Adley's hair and peered down at the box.

There were old foggers, scrapers and a bunch of other tools Nate couldn't identify. They were rusted and covered in water spots.

"These are probably from the 1910s," Grandpa said as he lifted out one of the foggers. He turned it over and showed it to them. Scrawled on the bottom it said "Michael Wilson, 1915." "My great-grandpa risked everything to turn his dairy farm to a honey farm. I remember my grandpa said that Michael had to fight his father, who thought Michael was a fool, since this is such good dairy cow farmland. Michael used all of his savings to purchase these tools, along with his first colonies, and started this business. He said he was doing it for the future generations of Wilsons who would own this farm." He shook his head in wonder. "Makes a man kind of feel special to know that his ancestor invested in him, not even knowing who he'd be."

Nate had never thought much about his Grandpa or Great-Grandpa Marshall. He didn't know much about his dad's dad, other than his name. Had the men in the Marshall family invested in Nate's life? It would be hard to know, since Nate's dad had taken whatever legacy he might have had with him the day he left.

What would it be like to be raised by men of integrity and character, who stuck around when the going got rough? Would Nate run if things got hard? Was that the legacy his family gave to the men who came after them—to disappear when life wasn't fun anymore?

"Now you two are part of that investment," Grandpa said, looking up at Adley and Benny—but he surprised Nate by gazing at him, too. "Actually—" he chuckled "—the three of you."

Adley put her arm around Grandpa Jed and smiled. "Thank you for keeping the legacy alive."

"No, Adley." He winked at her. "Thank you."

Nate would have felt like he was intruding on a moment, but they both looked up at him.

"And we have Nate to thank, too," Adley said. "If it wasn't for him, I wouldn't have even attempted to clean this barn out or say yes to the committee."

"I heartily agree." Grandpa put the fogger back into the crate. "Toss, donate or sell?"

"How about we save it?" Adley asked. "Nate had a great idea. He said we should save all the things that are unique to this farm and display them here in the barn when it's all cleaned."

Grandpa Jed chuckled as he shook his head. "One man's junk is another man's treasure, I guess."

"That saying has never been truer than now." Adley uncovered an antique tandem bike, in near perfect condition. It was painted red, and though the paint had faded with time and the tires had long since lost their air, it was beautiful.

"I remember that bike!" Grandpa walked over to Adley, his eyes shining with wonder. "That belonged to my parents. They loved to take this out at the end of the day, just the two of them, to enjoy the evening together. They'd often stay out until sunset and come back, windblown and happy. Boy, those two were in love. Made me excited for a relationship like that someday."

"And you had it with your Clara," Adley said with a tender smile.

"Sure did!" Grandpa grinned. "If I had known this was in here, I would have taken it out, shined it up and brought Clara out for an evening ride from time to time."

The three of them admired the bike for a bit.

"It's almost impossible to know what to do with all of this stuff," Adley said to both men. "Almost all of it will have memories attached to it. We can't save everything."

"No," Nate said, "but you can save the things that mean the most. I think this bike is one of them, don't you? I could drop it off at the bike repair shop and see what they could do with it."

Adley looked at Grandpa Jed. "Would you like that?"

"I don't know what I'll do with it, but it would make me happy every time I see it."

"We can hang it on some hooks, if you'd like." Nate pointed toward the far wall. "It would be out of the way and still be here for you to enjoy."

"That's a good thought." Grandpa patted one of the old seats. "Let's put it aside for now and see how many other treasures we find. If we have more than we want to keep, I can prioritize later."

"That sounds like a great plan." Nate removed the bike and started a new pile next to the barn.

The day continued in much the same vein. Nate loved hearing stories of the farm and the Wilson family. In a way, it made him feel like he was a part of the legacy, especially when Grandpa and Adley included him.

It was getting harder and harder to think about life after the Honeybee Ball.

Nate wasn't eager to leave.

# Chapter Ten

Adley stood in the middle of the clean barn, amazed at the progress they had made in the past two weeks. It was almost impossible to believe that they had sorted and emptied the barn, sold off the pieces that would bring in the most money and sent the rest to an antique shop that would sell their things on commission. Adley had already put the money they'd earned into their savings account. It felt good knowing they had a little set aside for the winter.

Light poured into the barn from the open doors and the electrical lights they'd had installed the past week. The barn had never been equipped with electricity, since it had been used for storage, but it was now ready to use both day and night. They had fixed broken and rotten boards, cleaned out cobwebs and old animal nests, and whitewashed everything until it shone. They hadn't had a chance to decorate with the antiques they had saved, but they'd get to that before the ball in a couple of weeks. The signs, the tandem bike and the other miscellaneous items rested against a far wall.

Today was the inspection, and Adley was so nervous, she hadn't been able to eat breakfast. She'd sent Benny to spend the day with her mom, freeing her up to give her full attention to the committee, who would arrive at any moment.

"What are you thinking about?" Nate asked as he appeared at the open door and leaned against the doorframe. "Did we forget anything?"

Adley looked around the barn again, admiring their hard work, and shook her head. They had painted several of the outbuildings, repaired all the broken windows and missing shingles, weeded the pumpkin patch, cleaned up the debris outside, and polished the processing room until it shone. The house had even been pressure-washed, and Nate had cleaned the old, leaded windows.

"Honestly, I don't remember this farm ever looking so good," she said. "There's always more we can do, but I think this is going to be as good as it gets for now."

Nate entered the building, with Sommer close to his side, and let his gaze wander over the large, almost-empty space. "I can't believe I've been here a month. Seems like I just arrived yesterday."

"We've done a lot in a month." Adley's gaze was caught on Nate, and her heart swelled with gratitude. "I couldn't have done any of this without you—truly. You've far surpassed any promise you made to Benjamin. I don't think I'll every properly be able to thank you—or repay you."

"You don't need to do either. I can see it in your face, Adley. Just knowing that I've helped you and Benny and Grandpa—it's all the payment I'll ever need." He put his hands in his pockets as he looked toward the open doors and the driveway beyond. "I guess I should start thinking about what I'm going to do after I leave. You won't have much need of me once the ball is done."

His words made her heart feel funny. They'd been so busy she hadn't thought much about what would happen after the ball. Most of the honey harvest was finished, and the colonies were due to ship out in a few weeks. A deep, piercing sadness overcame her at the thought of saying goodbye to him. She *did* have need of him—they all did. His presence on the farm had become something she not only relied upon but enjoyed. He'd easily slipped into his place among their little family, as if he belonged.

She swallowed the emotions, not knowing what to say. There was a part of her that wanted to tell him to stay—but to what end? She couldn't pay him what he was worth, and she couldn't ask him to give up whatever dreams he might have for his own future. A home, a career—a family? Nate was young and smart and talented. He could never settle for being a hired hand on a farm, especially one that was paid minimum wage or less. He'd be wasting his potential.

Yet the thought of him leaving gave her an ache in her chest.

"Do you think you'll go back to construction?" she asked, knowing she needed to say something.

"I've actually been thinking more about marketing. I really enjoyed working on your company brand. I used a part of my brain I haven't exercised in a while, but it all came back fast." He picked up the tennis ball Sommer dropped at his feet and threw it out into the barnyard. "I'm actually thinking about starting up my own business. I have a little money set aside that I can live on for a while, until my company gets up and running."

"I suppose you'll want to live in the Twin Cities, if you're going to make a go of a marketing business."

He shrugged. "With everything online, there's really no reason for me to live in the metro. I could live just about anywhere."

She swallowed and watched as Sommer chased her ball. "Where do you want to live?"

He didn't say anything for a moment, and Adley looked his way. He was watching her, his eyes asking a question she wasn't sure she wanted to answer.

"I promised you I would be honest," he said slowly, "no matter how hard the conversation, right?"

She nodded, her pulse picking up speed at the look in his eyes.

A car turned into the driveway, and Sommer started to bark.

Adley forced herself to tear her gaze away from Nate. "Sorry. I need to calm Sommer down before she scares the committee."

"Go ahead." He smiled. "We'll talk later."

She didn't want to leave him, but there was no choice. Adley left the barn and called for Sommer. Thankfully, the dog listened and trotted toward Adley as she waited for the vehicle to enter the barnyard.

Grandpa Jed must have been watching for the committee, because he exited the house wearing a clean button-down shirt and a pair of trousers that he had painstakingly ironed the night before. His clean-shaven face shone with pride as he made his way toward Adley.

"You did good, kiddo," he said to her as he met her smile with his own. "Even if they don't give us the grant, I'm proud of all you and Nate have accomplished. I can't remember this place looking so nice in all my life. And that's the truth."

She touched his arm with affection and then turned her gaze to the newcomers.

Three individuals exited the dark sedan, all of them looking around the farm with anticipation. Adley wished she knew what their first impressions were—and who they were competing against for the grant. It wouldn't change things, but perhaps she could get a better handle on whether or not they would win.

"Hello," said the woman who stepped out of the passenger side. "Are you Jed and Adley?"

"We are," Grandpa Jed said, standing up straighter as he looked from the lady to Adley.

"I'm Ruthann Olson, and these are my fellow committee members, Harry Jensen and Thomas Reed."

Adley greeted everyone and then noticed Nate was standing back near the barn. She motioned for him to join the group.

"This is one of our employees," Adley said, though "employee" was a loose term, since they hadn't paid Nate anything for his time. But she wasn't sure how else to introduce him. "Nate Marshall."

"It's nice to meet you, Nate," Ruthann said with a pleasant smile. She turned back to Adley and Grandpa Jed. "As we said in our initial letter, letting you know you are a finalist for this year's grant, we have a checklist we'll be working with today as we inspect your farm. Among other things we take into consideration is the age of the farm, giving extra consideration to farms that have withstood the test of time and have left a legacy in Minnesota. We look at the grant as a kind of investment in the future of honey production in the state. We want to know that the farm that wins will be around for a long, long time.

"We'll ask about your honey output, we'll inspect the health of your colonies, look at your processing room and do an overall inspection of the rest of your farm. It's really a painless process, but it's important since the grant winner is also considered the Honeybee Farm of the Year. If you win, you'll be highlighted in several magazines, on our website and in regional newspapers."

"Winning has its bonuses," Thomas said, "besides the obvious grant money."

Adley nodded her understanding, swallowing the nerves racing up her throat.

"We also want to say, at the outset," Harry told them, "that we appreciate your willingness to host the Honeybee Ball. We're eager to see the barn, and we want you to know that we will be working closely with you to provide tables and chairs, catering, portable outhouses and the like."

"I read that in the letter," Adley said. "We're just happy we could provide the space."

"Shall we get started?" Ruthann asked.

Adley thought it best to begin in the barn—and when she turned them in that direction, Ruthann stopped midstride. "Would you look at that stunning lake? Wow. That will be a nice backdrop for the ball, won't it?" she asked her fellow committee members, who heartily agreed.

It took over an hour for them to go through the farm. The committee was thorough, curious and easy to talk to. Grandpa Jed regaled them with stories from his youth, while Adley spoke about their hopes and dreams for the future. She told them about Benjamin and little Benny, and she told them what an honor it was to carry on the Wilson legacy.

Nate was also present to show them the new packaging he'd designed and the rebranded website he had created. The committee was deeply impressed, and Thomas asked Nate if he'd be willing to work on the website for the Minnesota Association of Beekeepers, giving Nate his first paying job for his new business.

As the committee pulled out of the driveway, Adley reached out and laid her hand on Grandpa Jed's arm again. Relief and excitement made her feel almost giddy. "I think that went well, don't you?"

"Better than I could have hoped." Grandpa Jed's blue eyes were shining as he looked from Adley to Nate. "You two make a great team, you know that?"

Adley turned to Nate and met his smile with one of her own. Something tender passed between them, and Adley had the urge to throw herself into his arms. They *did* make a good team—and always had. He occupied a special place in her heart, and that spot was expanding with each passing day. It wasn't a passionate, all-consuming feeling, but a gentle, quiet, steady one.

Yet life had taken a course of its own. Their paths had diverged, and for a long time, Adley had told herself she was okay with that. But now? When their paths had come back together, and she realized how much she had missed him and how well they still got along, would she be okay if they went their separate ways again? What were her other options? Something was happening to her heart, and she couldn't let it—not with Nate. Nothing had changed. If anything, she felt more guilt over betraying Benjamin's memory with each passing day.

"You deserve a day off," Grandpa Jed said to Adley. "Benny is at your mom's, and the big inspection is over. The harvest is done, and we have a couple weeks before the ball. The sky's the limit, so what do you want to do?"

"Honestly?" Adley appreciated that Grandpa Jed had taken her thoughts away from Nate and put them back on the right track. "I'd like to take a nap."

Grandpa and Nate both laughed, but Adley was serious.

"Well," Grandpa said, "after the nap, I think you should take yourself out for supper so you don't have to worry about cooking or cleaning tonight."

"You don't want to come with me?" she asked.

"Nah. I was thinking about going over to the Westermanns' and playing a game of chess with Hank tonight. Stella said she'd make me her famous beef stew." Grandpa nodded at Nate. "I want the two of you to go on without me. Get lost for the evening and forget all about your troubles."

Adley glanced at Nate again, wondering if it was a good idea to go out alone with him. It sounded an awful lot like a date.

"What do you say?" Nate asked her. "We could go to Ruby's Bistro and then catch a movie at the Falls Cinema. Or we could walk down by the river—whatever you'd like to do." He paused. "Unless you'd rather not have me tag along. I could just as easily stay here and heat up some leftovers."

"I'm not going to ask you to eat leftovers." She shook her head at him, smiling. "I think we should definitely go out and celebrate all this hard work we've done. And it'll be my treat."

"Now, wait a minute, boss," Nate said. "I'm not in the habit of letting the young lady pay for supper. If we're going, let's do it properly." He stood up straight and affected a serious tone.

"I'll call for you at six o'clock, sharp—and I don't want to see you carrying your wallet."

Adley chuckled, happy to keep the mood light and carefree. "You got it, Natertot."

They laughed all the way back to the house, and as Adley climbed the stairs for that promised nap, she couldn't help but look forward to a night out with Nate. Even if she had warning bells going off in her mind and heart.

The evening had turned cool as Nate stepped out of the truck in downtown Timber Falls. He should have been excited, but he felt too nervous to enjoy himself. Not only was he going to have Adley all to himself for the next couple of hours, but he had promised her that they would talk about what was on his mind. And he didn't know how she would feel about what he had to say.

Over the past month, Nate's feelings for Adley had grown deeper, if that was possible. It was more than attraction he felt for her, more than affection or friendship. Adley was unlike anyone he'd ever known. She fit perfectly beside him. Their personalities complemented each other, and he loved being with her. Not only did they work well as a team, like Grandpa Jed had said, but he knew that they could work well as more than business partners.

He wanted to stay in Timber Falls and continue to see what, if anything, could come from their relationship. He didn't want to watch Benny grow up from a distance, or return to the Twin Cities and be lost in a crowd of people who didn't know him or really care that much about him. His roots were here, in Timber Falls, with Adley, and he wanted to plant them and watch them grow.

The guilt he carried for what he had said to Adley the day before her wedding had started to fade. It had been a mistake, but he hadn't done it to hurt her or Benjamin. And he couldn't deny that Benjamin had asked him to come back and help Adley and Benny. Wasn't that like forgiveness? If Benjamin had been able to see past Nate's mistake, could Adley?

Hope mingled with anticipation—yet everything hinged on Adley. It was hard to know her thoughts and feelings. She had kept them close since he'd returned to the farm, and he didn't blame her. They'd been busy and preoccupied—but now, most of it was behind them.

Adley stepped out of the other side of the truck and looked up at Ruby's Bistro. The large plate-glass windows were decorated with a fall theme, and up and down Main Street, there were cornstalks, pumpkins and scarecrows in many of the other business windows. Fall was fast approaching, bringing with it the cooler temps, the hint of burning leaves and the promise of longer evenings. Winter wasn't too far behind, and Nate wanted to have a better feel for where he might be by the time the snow flew.

But would that be here, in his hometown, or in an apartment, several stories above Minneapolis?

They entered Ruby's Bistro and were shown to a booth along the side of the restaurant. It was an eclectic space, decorated with a large pastoral mural painted on one wall by a local artist, as well as relics from Timber Falls' past. There was the old drive-in theater sign, a drugstore marquee, a diner sign and more. "Retro elegance" was a term Nate had heard others use to describe Ruby's style.

After the waitress took their orders, Nate smiled across the table at Adley.

She smiled, too, but there was reservation in her gaze.

"What's wrong?" he asked.

"I don't know. I kind of feel guilty or something."

"Guilty?" He frowned. "Why?"

"This is the first time I've gone out to eat without Benny since he was born. I feel free—but also kind of lonely, if that's possible."

Affection warmed his heart, and he had to resist the urge to reach out and touch her hand. "You deserve a little break from time to time. I'm just happy I could be the one to enjoy it with you."

Her face became serious as she leaned forward. "You are a lifesaver, Nate. I know it's getting old to hear, but thank you, from the bottom of my heart. I'm so grateful you showed up when you did."

He needed to tread carefully, inspect the water before he dived beneath the surface. "So you're not upset that I didn't honor my promise and stay away?"

She studied him for a moment. "I'm happy Benjamin asked you to come—and I'm glad that you did."

"So am I." He took a deep breath. "Earlier, I started to tell you something, before the committee came."

"I remember."

Her hands were clasped on the table as she leaned toward him. Slowly, he reached out and put one of his hands over hers.

She looked down at his hand, but she didn't pull away. Instead, she turned her beautiful green gaze to his with a question in its depth.

"I'm so happy we've rekindled our friendship, Adley. I know I don't deserve a second chance, but you've given me one, and I never want to say or do anything to hurt it again."

"Nate." She swallowed as she began to shake her head. "I—"

"Adley?" Rick Johnson came to a sudden halt next to their table. He looked down at their hands, and then he sent Nate a cold glare.

"Dad." Adley removed her hand and leaned back in the booth. "What are you doing here?"

Spencer approached the table, a wide grin on his face. "Hi, Adley."

"Hi, Spencer." Adley motioned to Nate. "You remember Nate."

Spencer nodded but didn't say anything.

"We're here for a dinner meeting," Rick said to his daughter. "What are you doing here?"

Taking a deep breath, Adley put on a forced smile. "Celebrating."

Rick narrowed his eyes. "Oh? Something I should be aware of? Don't tell me you've completely lost your mind and plan to get married."

Anger flared to life in Nate's chest, and he had to breathe through his nose as he clenched his jaw together.

"You're not, are you?" Rick asked. "It would be the biggest mistake of your life. Nate doesn't have any prospect or potential. Not like Spencer, here."

Spencer took a step back and lifted his hands. "I'll see you at the office tomorrow, Rick."

If Nate could have left, he would have. He'd never been more insulted in his life, yet what could he say or do to defend himself? The last thing he wanted was to make a scene and embarrass Adley.

"You have no idea who Nate is," Adley said to her father, keeping her voice calm, though Nate could tell it wasn't easy for her.

"It's okay, Adley," Nate said. "You don't need to defend me."

"You're wrong." Adley looked back at her dad. "I've never met someone more honorable or trustworthy or hardworking as Nate Marshall. He showed up when no one else did, and he put his future on hold to make sure that Benny and I have one."

Nate loved Adley all the more for defending him, but he knew why her dad was making such claims. Nate wasn't that much younger than Spencer, yet their lives and bank accounts were probably as different as night and day. If Rick judged a man based on financial success, then he would find Nate lacking.

"Calm down, Adley," Rick said. "As long as

you don't plan to marry this guy, I could care less how honorable he is."

"His honor is important. He is a soldier and was deployed last year, serving our country selflessly."

"Adley." Nate reached for her hand. "It's not necessary. I don't have anything to prove to your dad." It wasn't true, but he didn't want Rick Johnson to know how much he cared about the other man's opinion. He was Adley's father, and there was a part of him that wanted Rick to like him, especially since his own father had abandoned him—but he wouldn't give Rick the satisfaction of knowing how much.

Adley swallowed and lifted her chin. "I don't think we have anything else to say to each other, Dad."

Rick twisted the class ring he wore on his right hand. "Actually, I was planning to talk to you when you stopped by to pick up your son. Spencer and I came up with a solid price for your farm, and the couple who are interested have agreed to it. All you need to do is sign a purchase agreement, and you'll have more money than you could imagine. You can buy a nice house here in town for you and Benny and get on with your life."

Adley frowned at her dad. "You don't get it,

do you? I *have* gone on with my life. I'm doing exactly what I want, and Benny and I are perfectly fine with the way things are. In fact, I have no wish for anything to change. I like things just as they are right now."

Her words, coupled with Rick's, burned a hole in Nate's heart and destroyed his hope. He was a fool to think that she could ever love him the way he loved her. Even if her dad wasn't part of the equation, he still had to think about Benny and the farm—not to mention Adley's relationship with Benjamin and her hopes for the future. She had been in a bad place when he had come, but she was on her way out. The farm would prosper, and she and Benny would be just fine on their own. There wasn't anything she couldn't do, and she could do it without him.

"I told the couple that you probably wouldn't make up your mind until after the harvest," Rick said, "so you have some time to think it over."

He didn't wait for her to respond but turned and left the restaurant.

Adley briefly closed her eyes and took a few steadying breaths before she looked at Nate. "I'm sorry—he was way out of line and completely wrong about you. I'm so embarrassed."

"It's okay, Adley. I don't need your father's approval." Again—it wasn't true. He wanted it more than anything. He wanted Adley's dad to like him.

She studied him with a look that said she didn't quite believe him, but she let it go. "I can't think straight. What were we talking about?"

"Nothing important," he said with a sad smile.

As the waitress approached with their drinks, Nate resolved that he wouldn't say anything to Adley about his feelings for her. He'd made a mess of it last time, and it had been the biggest regret of his life. He valued their friendship too much to make the same mistake twice. It was better if he made plans to return to the Twin Cities and put this part of his life behind him.

It would be best for everyone.

# Chapter Eleven

Adley could hardly believe two weeks had passed and the Minnesota Association of Beekeepers Convention was well underway. Timber Falls was a perfect place to host the event, with its central location and beautiful Riverview Convention Center on the banks of the Mississippi River. Adley and Grandpa had been attending the workshops and breakout sessions for two days. Dozens of vendors and national experts were on hand to answer questions, share knowledge and demonstrate the newest technology. It was exciting to be a part of something Adley felt so passionate about. The more she learned about the honey industry, the more certain she was that she was in this for the long haul.

It wasn't the career she had sought, but it was the one that had found her.

"I don't know about you," Grandpa Jed said from beside her in the pickup truck on the way home from the second day of the convention, "but I am ready to get some shut-eye."

Adley tried to stifle her yawn as she smiled at Grandpa. The country road was dark, hiding the brilliance of the autumn leaves lining the road. The last thing she wanted him to know was that she wouldn't be going to bed any time soon. Tomorrow evening was the Honeybee Ball, and there was still a lot to do. She didn't know when she'd get to go to bed. Thankfully, her mom had enjoyed spending the day with Benny a couple weeks ago and had offered to take him for the duration of the three-day convention. Adley had never been away from him for so long, but she had spoken to her mom several times in the past two days and all seemed to be going well. It was probably because Adley's dad had been out of town on business. She doubted he would be happy to share his house with a seven-month-old baby.

"We have another early morning with the final keynote address," Adley told Grandpa Jed. "And then the ball tomorrow evening. You need to get your sleep so you have energy to dance with me."

Grandpa laughed and patted her arm. "I don't

think you'll need me to dance with you—not when you have Nate."

He said it so calmly, so matter-of-fact, that Adley's thoughts came to a pause.

Ever since the night they had gone to Ruby's Bistro together, Nate had been keeping his distance. They had worked side by side every day on the barn and the rest of the farm, but he had become withdrawn and quiet around her. When she had asked Grandpa Jed if he had noticed anything a few days ago, he said no. Nate was just fine around him. Adley couldn't help but worry that Nate's behavior was a direct result of her father's comments. The change had happened that very night, and it was too coincidental not to be related.

But every time Adley had tried to talk to him about her father's words, Nate had avoided the discussion, making excuses to leave the room or get busy doing something else. Adley had been too preoccupied with the Honeybee Ball preparations to dig deeper, hoping and praying that eventually Nate would open up with her— so far, he hadn't.

Grandpa Jed let out a sad sigh. "It's going to be awfully quiet around the farm without Nate. I've grown so used to him being there. I don't know what I'll do when he's gone."

His words mirrored the same thoughts she'd been having the past two weeks.

They were both silent for a minute, and then Grandpa said, "Have you talked to him about his plans? He'll be leaving the day after tomorrow, won't he?"

"As far as I know, he's planning to return to the Twin Cities."

"That's what he said?"

"I haven't heard otherwise." A car was approaching from the opposite direction, so Adley turned off her bright lights. "We haven't had much time to talk."

"How do you feel about that?"

"What? Not having time to talk?"

"Him going to the Cities."

"What does it matter how I feel? Nate has a life to live, and he needs to do what's best for him."

"He's not a city guy. He's a small-town man—maybe even a farmer."

Adley swallowed the nerves that fluttered in her throat at Grandpa's insinuation, but she didn't want to assume. "What are you trying to say, Grandpa?"

"That if Nate wanted to stay on at the farm, I would like that—a whole lot."

"You know we can't pay him to stay. Even

with the new income we're taking in, it's not enough to hire someone full time."

Grandpa was quiet for a moment, and Adley could feel his gaze on her. "I wasn't suggesting you offer him a job."

If she hadn't been driving, she would have tried to study his face to catch his meaning without needing to ask. Up ahead, the farm came within sight and the barn was lit up. She hadn't expected to see the lights on. It was late, and she had assumed Nate would have gone to bed already. Was he still awake?

"Well?" Grandpa asked.

"Well, what?"

"Do you want him to stay?"

"What are you getting at, Grandpa?"

He let out a frustrated breath. "Do you like him or not, Adley?"

Adley's mouth slipped open, and she did look at him as she slowed down to pull into the driveway. "Like him?"

"Okay—love him? Do you love Nate? I might be old and hard of hearing, but I'm not blind. I see how you two look at each other. I've always seen it. To be honest, I was a little surprised that you chose Benjamin back in high school. I was thrilled that you chose him, mind you— but surprised."

"Grandpa, Benjamin is my husband. I could never betray him with his best friend."

"Betray him?" Grandpa pulled his head back. "Your wedding vows said until death do you part. As hard as it is to accept, you're no longer wedded to Benjamin. You're free to move on with your life—and you should."

"Why didn't you ever remarry then?" She was throwing up a smoke screen, trying to get him off the topic at hand, especially as they were now in the yard and she could see Nate working in the barn. She didn't want to be talking about this with Grandpa right now.

"That's different," Grandpa Jed said. "I'm old and set in my ways. When Clara died, I was almost seventy. I knew there wasn't anyone who would be willing to saddle themselves to me. But you're different. You're young and full of life. It's a shame to be wasting it at this farm with an old codger like me."

"You're not an old codger." She put the truck in Park and turned off the engine. "And I'm already set in my ways, too." She tried to laugh, but he just shook his head.

"How long will you punish yourself, Adley?"

Her smile disappeared. "Punish myself?"

"I lived here when you and Benjamin were first married. I tried not to eavesdrop, but I know things weren't good, and I suspect that Nate had something to do with it."

Remorse and guilt filled Adley's stomach, and she looked down at her hands, barely croaking out, "You knew?"

"I knew enough." He patted her hand. "Every marriage has its obstacles. Mine certainly did. I know you questioned if you'd done the right thing by marrying Benjamin, but you're definitely not the first bride to doubt. I also know that you were committed to your husband and you two had finally worked it out."

Adley's chest rose and fell on the swell of emotions raging through her.

"And I also know that God is sovereign," Grandpa continued, in a gentler voice. "For whatever reason, He took Benjamin and gave Nate. Don't let the past dictate your future. Don't let your regrets force you to live in the past. You loved Benjamin, and he loved you. You were always faithful to him, and you have nothing to be ashamed of or feel guilty about. Thoughts are not actions. Even if you wrestled with your doubts, you never dishonored your husband."

What he said was true. Adley had been faithful to Benjamin. She had nothing to feel guilty about.

"If you love Nate," Grandpa said, "don't let

anything stand in your way—and that's the free advice you get from a guy who has lived a lot longer than he deserves."

Adley reached over and gave him a hug. His words resonated with her heart, but she needed time to think about what they meant for her future. A part of her wanted to accept what he said—that she was free to love Nate. But another part—a big part—was still tethered to the memory of Benjamin and she didn't know how long it would be until she could untie the knots.

"I love you," Adley said to Grandpa. "Thank you."

"No matter what you decide, you have my blessing. I just wanted you to know that I would wholeheartedly welcome Nate as a permanent part of the family—if that's what you want."

After Adley pulled away from him, he opened his door and paused. "Need any more help tonight?"

"Head on in to bed. I'll just go and see what Nate is doing and if he needs anything before I turn in."

"Okay. Good night."

"Night, Grandpa."

As Grandpa moved toward the house, Adley stepped out of the pickup truck and walked toward the barn. The dark autumn sky was crisp with millions of sparkling stars overhead. All around, the night sounds played like a gentle melody. Crickets sang, the wind whistled and the frogs croaked. The air was cool, and the forecast promised to be perfect for the ball tomorrow night.

During the dance, they would also have a bonfire and hayrides for their guests. Steve and Paul had volunteered to come out and make sure both ran smoothly. The hay wagon stood off to the side of the barn, ready to go, while the wood for the fire was stacked up on the other side, between the barn and the lake. The pumpkins were ready to harvest, and the apples were ripe on the trees. Adley planned to make applesauce, apple butter and apple juice in the weeks after the ball.

There was always work to do on the farm, and though she looked forward to all of it, she couldn't deny that she felt melancholy thinking about life after Nate left. She could see herself picking apples with him and Benny, carving pumpkins, raking leaves—everything felt more exciting and joyful with him nearby. But once he left, it would be just her and Benny doing those things together—and maybe Grandpa on his good days.

A pang of homesickness overtook her as she

came up to the barn doors. Strange, since she was home. Was she feeling this emotion thinking about Nate being gone? Had he become home?

He was on a ladder, attaching a string of white lights to a hook in the corner of the barn. His speaker was on a table, playing a popular song from their high school years. It made her long for those simpler times.

"Hey," he said when he saw her. "I hope you don't mind that I added some lights."

Adley's head tipped back as she walked under the lights and looked up to the tall ceiling. The sparkling strands were suspended midway in the air, reminding her of the millions of stars outside.

"I love them."

He finished hooking the lights and then climbed down the ladder. He was wearing a simple pair of blue jeans and a white T-shirt. His hair was a little longer than it had been six weeks ago when he arrived. It curled at the tips and looked windblown tonight.

But it was his brown eyes, shining under the glow of the twinkle lights, that captured her attention. He was so handsome and strong and confident. But more than that, he was kind and good and thoughtful. He was the first person she wanted to see each morning and the last one she wanted to see at night. Nate was the man she wanted to sit on the front porch with and talk about life, the one she wanted to share her highs and lows with, and entrust with her home, her child and her heart.

In that moment, she knew she was in love with him, and that the love she felt for him now was much different than the love she had felt for him before. She had always cared about Nate. He had been her dear friend. The schoolgirl crush she'd had on him was only that—a crush. When she had married Benjamin, she had been in love with Benjamin. She hadn't been in love with Nate back then.

But now? Now she was in love with Nate. In the past month and a half, something had shifted and changed within her heart, going deeper and wider. Her love for him had grown and was now so much bigger than she knew what to do with.

Suddenly, her fear that he had come to rekindle his feelings for her became her fear that he hadn't. Was that why he was avoiding a conversation between them?

Nate hadn't expected to see Adley tonight. He'd assumed that she and Grandpa Jed would have gone into the house together. So when he turned around and saw her standing in the open doorway, underneath the twinkling lights, his breath had caught. She was beautiful, with her dark hair around her shoulders, wearing nice clothes for the conference. Ever since the inspection, she had seemed like a different person—the old Adley. She was more relaxed and less overwhelmed. And he suspected that even if she didn't get the grant, she felt like she had a better handle on her life.

Her newfound peace was yet more confirmation that she would be better off without him. He'd tried for two weeks to avoid being in private, intimate moments with her—moments like this one. He'd been so close to telling her how he felt at Ruby's Bistro, but he was confident that it would have been a mistake. If he'd learned anything in life it was that timing was everything, and declaring his love for someone who didn't return his feelings was just about the worst experience he could imagine.

He wanted to excuse himself and go in to bed—but he didn't want to be rude. "How was the second day of the convention?"

"It was amazing. I feel so energized to tackle this business. If we win the grant, I can pay off the remainder of our debt and then turn my focus to better things. Grandpa and I have talked about expanding our colonies and ramping up our production. Sales from the past two weeks have tripled, thanks to your new labels and website. If they keep up, I'm afraid we won't have enough honey to meet the demand."

"That's amazing, Adley." He was happy for her.

She was wearing a long jacket, cinched at the waist, over a pair of ankle-length pants and heels. Her outfit was a far cry from what she usually wore around the farm, but he liked both styles on her. She was always pretty.

Now she put her hands in her pockets and pressed her lips together for a moment, as if she was contemplating whether or not she should say whatever she was thinking.

Finally, she plunged ahead. "Grandpa Jed and I were just talking about you."

"Yeah? I hope it was something good."

She smiled, and his heart did a funny little flip.

Would she always make him feel this way?

"Of course it was something good." Her face became serious then, and he had the urge to rub away the worry lines, allowing her to smile again. "Grandpa and I both agree that we don't want to see you leave."

A silly part of him had wished she had said

"*I* don't want to see you leave." But what would it matter? He had forced himself to come to terms with the reality that his life was going to go on without Adley Wilson. Her father's words had taunted him for two weeks, and he knew that she would be better off with someone like Spencer—someone who was steady and successful. She didn't need the instability he would bring to her life—she had enough of that already. He was trying to start up a business and didn't even have a dependable income. And if that wasn't bad enough, he had his past mistakes to chase him for the rest of his life. Her dad was right. He was a bad choice for Adley and always had been.

He laid his hammer down on the worktable with his speaker and turned off the music. It was a song that had always reminded him of Adley, and right now it was just too painful to hear. "I'm happy I was able to help when you needed me. But I think you and Grandpa Jed have a good handle on things now. I'll check in from time to time, and don't be afraid to ask for help whenever you need it. Minneapolis isn't far."

She studied him, her eyes filled with a myriad of emotions. "So, you're moving to Minneapolis then?"

"I found an apartment online and plan to check it out the day after tomorrow. If it's not a good fit, I'll crash with a buddy of mine for a few days until I can find something else."

"Oh." She lowered her gaze and grabbed the ends of her jacket belt. "That makes sense. You'll grow your business a lot faster there if you're able to make connections in person."

Her voice didn't sound happy for him—she sounded sad and disappointed. Did she really want him to stay? His heart started to beat faster at the thought. But did she want him to stay because he'd been good for the farm—or because he had been good for her? He wished he could believe such a thing, but the past was a pretty good indicator of the future and he'd never been good for her. Benjamin had always been the better man, and she had chosen wisely. Just because Benjamin wasn't here didn't mean that Nate was now the best choice.

He was starting to feel confused and messed up inside. One part of him wanted to pull Adley close and ask her if she wanted him to stay. The other part wanted to run as far and as fast as he could, not willing to open himself up to the pain he'd felt the last time she rejected him.

All he needed to do was remind himself that he wasn't good enough for her. Her dad took the opportunity to do it as often as possible, so it wasn't hard to convince himself it was true.

"It's getting pretty late," he said. "We have a big day ahead of us."

She simply nodded, still watching him, as if trying to discern what he was thinking.

He couldn't let her know his thoughts. He had to keep them shut deep inside, just like he always had.

Nate moved to the bank of light switches and paused. "Are you heading inside, or do you want me to leave the lights on for you?"

"I'll go inside. It looks like you took care of all the little odds and ends I was going to deal with tonight."

He flipped the lights off, one by one, until it was dark inside the barn.

The only light now came from the stars and moon.

Adley helped him close the large barn doors, and then they walked toward the house together.

"For what it's worth," Adley said right after she opened the back door to enter the house, "I'm going to miss you, more than I thought possible. I've loved having you be a part of my life again."

He took the door from her to hold it open.

Without warning, she stood on tiptoe and laid a kiss against his cheek.

The touch of her lips was so soft, and so gentle, he inhaled and couldn't breathe for a second. He was stunned—and by the time he realized what had happened, she had turned away and was gone upstairs, leaving him to stand there like a besotted fool.

Nate had to swallow a couple of times to regain some sort of equilibrium, and then he entered the dark kitchen and walked through it as quietly as possible, so he wouldn't disturb Grandpa, who was probably asleep already.

He flipped on the lamp in the sunroom and slowly lowered himself onto the couch, still a little dazed by Adley's kiss.

Since leaving Timber Falls and joining the National Guard, he'd been kissed many times before—and with a lot more passion—but none of them had felt as intense as Adley's gentle kiss on the cheek. She had the ability to render him completely powerless, and she had no idea.

His heart started to thump harder as he thought about her words. She loved having him be a part of her life. She had said she'd miss him. Maybe, when she had said that she and Grandpa didn't want to see him leave, she had meant *she* didn't want him to leave, after all.

Yet even if her feelings for him had deepened, he still had to do what he thought was best for her. And he wasn't sure it was him.

His phone sat on the end table next to the couch charging. He hadn't had it with him that evening as he worked in the barn, so he picked it up to see what time it was, hoping it wasn't too late and he could still have time to talk to Adley tonight. Ask her what she meant.

But there was a voice message on his phone from a number he didn't recognize.

Nate pressed the voice mail icon and tapped the message, then he put his phone up to his ear to listen.

"Nate, this is Rick Johnson. I got your number from your mom. Look, I know we haven't always seen eye to eye, but I'd like your help. I think it would be mutually beneficial to both of us. The buyers who are interested in Adley's farm have just upped their offer, and it's substantial. They're serious and want to close this deal as soon as possible. Adley would have more than enough money to buy herself a nice house, somewhere in town, for her, Benny and Jed, with plenty left over to get her back on her feet. She'd be a fool not to at least consider this offer. Can you help her understand? If you can, I'll make it worth your while. This is really what's best for her, and I think you know that, too. Give me a call and I'll let you know the details."

Pulling the phone away from his ear, Nate stared at it for a minute in disgust. He wasn't sure what surprised him more: that Rick would assume he'd help him after all the times he'd been a jerk to Nate or that Rick didn't know his daughter well enough to know she'd never sell.

It was too late to call Rick and tell him—and too late to knock on Adley's door to chat.

But tomorrow, before the day was through, he'd have a heart-to-heart with her and tell her what was bothering him, no matter how uncomfortable it might be.

# Chapter Twelve

"Adley?" Grandpa Jed called up the stairs. "Are you ready yet?"

Adley opened her eyes and blinked a couple of times. For a second, she was confused, but then she lifted her phone off the bedside table and looked at the time. It took a moment for her eyes to adjust and then she finally saw that it was eight thirty—and almost had a panic attack.

She and Grandpa Jed should have been on their way to the convention center already! The morning session started at nine, and the master of ceremonies would be announcing the three finalists for the grant, expecting them to be on stage. They'd also remind everyone to come out to the Wilson farm for the dance that night to hear the winner announced.

With her heart pumping wildly, Adley jumped

out of bed and flew to the door to open it and call down to Grandpa. "I must have forgotten to set my alarm clock! I never sleep this late. I'll be down as fast as I can!"

"I'll be waiting out in the pickup truck."

Adley rushed to her closet and pulled out the first thing that looked decent, though it was wrinkled and a little out of fashion. She couldn't be picky this morning—not when she was running late.

She pulled the black dress over her head as she ran across the hallway to the small bathroom. There wasn't enough time to shower, but she did manage to brush her teeth as she put on a little mascara, then she quickly combed her hair as she went back to her room to throw some black flats on her feet. She found a jean jacket to toss on over the dress and grabbed her cell phone, throwing her comb on her unmade bed as she ran down the stairs.

"Whoa," Nate said as they collided in the kitchen.

He grabbed her by the shoulders so she wouldn't fall backward.

"Sorry," she said, breathing heavily. "I'm running late."

"I made breakfast. I was hoping we could have a talk."

"I'm so sorry." Embarrassment at her lack of responsibility warmed her cheeks. "I really have to go. We're expected on stage during the morning session." She was moving toward the door as she grabbed her purse and a set of keys.

"Here." He handed her the mug of coffee in his hand and grabbed a couple pieces of toast off a plate. "It's something to fill your stomach, at least. We can talk later."

His thoughtfulness warmed her heart. "Thank you. We won't be home until around suppertime. The tables and chairs should be delivered late this morning, but everything else will come around five. Do you mind telling the rental company where to unload?"

"I will be here all day to help anyone who needs help."

"Thank you." Her hands were full, so he came around her to open the door.

His hair was a little damp from his morning shower, and his face was freshly shaved. He smelled like soap and cologne. Adley wanted to take a deep breath, to keep that smell close all day, but decided to smile, instead. "We'll talk later, okay?"

"Okay." He held the door as she walked onto the back porch. "I hope you and Grandpa Jed have a great day. I'll see you later."

"Bye." She would have waved, but her hands were full.

Thankfully, Grandpa saw her coming and he jumped out of the truck and took her mug of coffee and her purse so she could open the driver's-side door.

She hated to speed, but the last thing she wanted was to be a no-show while they introduced the grant finalists. That wouldn't look good.

When they arrived at the convention center, she dropped Grandpa off at the door and told him to make a beeline for the stage door. Even if she couldn't get there on time, at least he'd be there to represent them.

Finally, she found a parking spot and sprinted to the entrance, arriving in the lobby right as the clock turned nine.

When she found the stage door, she was so out of breath, she had to take a moment to stop and breathe deeply.

"Are you one of the finalists?" a young man asked. He had an official name tag and a clipboard. He raised his eyebrows behind his glasses as he watched her catch her breath.

"I am Adley Wilson, yes."

"You were supposed to be here fifteen minutes ago to receive your instructions." He consulted his watch and then his piece of paper. "I don't know if you'll be able to go on now."

Disappointment made her feel weak. "Have they announced the finalists yet?"

"Not yet. They're just getting started."

"Then why can't I go on?"

"You weren't here for practice."

"Practice? What do I have to do but walk across the stage?"

"There are markers on the floor for you to stand on."

"Did Jed Wilson come through here?"

"Yes."

She was quickly losing patience with this boy. "Where is he?"

"Waiting to go on stage."

"He's only been here a few minutes longer than me."

"But I had time to give him instructions."

Adley put her hands over her face, trying hard to keep her cool. "How about I just do whatever he does? Will that work?"

The young man looked as if he was seriously considering her request. "Okay, but if you make a mistake, I don't want to be the one responsible."

"I'll be fine."

He shook his head as he opened the door and allowed Adley to enter the backstage area.

It was dark, but the light coming from the stage gave her the ability to make out Grandpa's figure. He motioned for her to join him.

"Do you know what we're doing?" she whispered to him.

Grandpa Jed just chuckled and nodded. "Walk on when they announce our name. Smile. And then walk off after the applause."

Adley still didn't know who they were up against for the grant. She looked at the other people standing backstage with them and didn't recognize anyone. There were almost a hundred honeybee farms in Minnesota, and she definitely wasn't familiar with all of them. Grandpa Jed had a better grasp of who was who, but even he didn't know everyone.

She smiled at the other people, and then it was time to go on stage.

"The first finalist for this year's grant and award as the Minnesota Honeybee Farm of the Year is Sweet Basil Honey Farms."

Adley lifted her eyebrows as a young couple, not much older than her, held hands as they left the shadows of backstage and stepped into the light.

For some reason, seeing them together, hand

in hand, gave her a pang in her heart. She loved Grandpa Jed, and was proud to be there with him, but she missed Benjamin. Missed having a partner to walk through life, hand in hand.

"We should have invited Nate to come," Grandpa Jed said. "He might have enjoyed being here at the convention, to learn a little more about the honey industry."

Nate might have enjoyed himself, but if he wasn't staying, what would be the point? Was it enough that she wanted him there?

She should have been listening to the MC giving all the details about Sweet Basil Honey Farms, but Adley's mind was on Nate and how much she had wanted to talk to him last night in the barn. Again, he had been distant and evasive—but what had he said this morning? He wanted to talk to her?

Adley's heart picked up speed, wondering what he wanted to talk about.

"Sweet Basil Honey Farms has been in the Stewart family since 1969," the MC said. "But it was just recently that Marcus Stewart and his wife, Vanessa, purchased the farm from Marcus's father. They changed the name to Sweet Basil Honey Farms just this year and completely revamped their branding." The MC went on about Marcus and Vanessa and their small family, carrying on the traditions of their forefathers.

Their story was similar to Adley's, though the Wilson farm had started producing honey several decades before the Stewart family—and instead of Benjamin and Adley running the farm, it was just Adley, with Grandpa Jed's help.

"This will be a close one," Grandpa whispered to Adley. "They seem like real nice folks."

Adley smiled and nodded.

After the next farm was announced, it was finally time for Adley and Grandpa Jed to step out onto the stage. As they walked toward the podium where the other families had stood while the MC read off their bio sheet, Adley belatedly realized she hadn't even looked in the mirror before she ran out of the house this morning. Instead of smiling confidently before the large auditorium and the inspection committee who was sitting in the front row, she felt self-conscious and uncomfortable. Her dress still had wrinkles, but did it look okay with the jean jacket? Did her hair look crazy? Had her makeup smudged?

Before long, it was over, and Adley and Grandpa were back in the hallway, breathing a sigh of relief.

"I'm going to go sit in the auditorium so I can

listen to the keynote address," Grandpa said. "Want to join me?"

"I think a visit to the ladies' room is in order first." She smiled. "Save me a seat, please."

"You got it, kiddo." He winked and then left her to find a spot to sit.

Adley walked down the hall to find the ladies' room, but before she could locate it, she noticed a familiar figure near one of the windows, on his phone.

He glanced up at her and waved in surprise, and then quickly ended his call to meet her in the hallway. "Hi, Adley. What are you doing here?"

"Hey, Spencer." She smiled, though she still was concerned about her appearance. "I'm here for the Minnesota Association of Beekeepers Convention."

"Of course you are." He tapped his forehead, as if he was a dunce. "I'm here for some meetings. Your dad is around here somewhere, too." He looked down the hall as if Dad would materialize on command.

Adley pointed over her shoulder with her thumb. "I should probably get back in there."

"Sure." He nodded and smiled. "I just thought it was such a cool coincidence to run into you, I couldn't ignore you."

"I agree." She started to back away, but his words stopped her.

"Your mom told me about the Honeybee Ball at your place tonight. It sounds pretty amazing."

"Yeah. It should be a lot of fun."

"Is everyone invited? Or do you have to be a member of the beekeepers' association to get a ticket?"

Adley wasn't sure if he was fishing for an invitation or if he was just being polite. "Anyone can come, I guess. Are you interested?"

"I'd love to be there." He slipped his cell phone into his back pocket. "I'm free later this afternoon. Do you need any help getting things ready?"

She considered all the work setting up the chairs and tables and found herself nodding. "If you'd like to help, I won't turn you away."

"Great. I'll head out there around suppertime."

"Perfect."

"Your dad also mentioned the good news."

"What good news?"

"That you're willing to accept the offer for your farm. I couldn't be happier. If you want the truth, you are getting the better end of the deal."

She stared at Spencer, unsure what to say. So instead of speaking, she just frowned.

Spencer also frowned. "Your dad said he talked to Nate."

"Nate?" Adley felt more confused than ever. "Why would my dad talk to Nate?"

"Apparently, Nate thought it was a good idea, so he spoke to your dad and said you had agreed to sell."

"Nate told my dad I would be willing to sell?" Adley was so confused.

"Wasn't that why he's been at your farm, helping you get everything in shape?"

"No." Adley shook her head. "At least, that's not why he said he was there."

"Oh. I guess I could be wrong, but your dad said Nate was there helping you get things ready to sell."

Adley's confusion continued to grow. Was that why Nate had come? To help get the place ready to sell? It didn't seem true—but why would Spencer say such a thing?

"I should let you get going," Spencer said. "I'll see you out at the farm this evening."

Nodding, Adley turned away. She pulled her cell phone out of her purse and called Nate, but he didn't answer.

Instead of focusing on the rest of the convention, all she could think about was getting home and asking Nate if there was any truth to what Spencer had just said.

Nate spent the day cleaning up the farmyard. The leaves were still hanging on the trees in a brilliant array of colors. A few were lying on the ground, but not enough for a full-blown fall cleanup. Instead, he took out the riding lawn mower and cut the grass. It was a big job and took him a couple of hours. He mowed parts of the yard that weren't usually cut, but with all the people they were expecting, he and Adley had agreed to make sure it was all nice and short.

After the grass was cut, he took out a large backpack blower and blew off the porch, the walkways and the driveway. When the rental company showed up with the chairs, tables and dance floor, he showed them where to unload. After a quick sandwich, he spent the rest of the afternoon on a project he'd been wanting to get done for a long time—one that hadn't been a top priority for the ball, but had a lot of meaning to him. When he was done, he went into the house to take a quick shower, since it was almost five and Adley was due to return any second.

He didn't want to have a rushed conversation

with her about the future, but he also didn't want to keep putting it off, either. Maybe today, with all their responsibilities and distractions, wasn't the best time to have such an important discussion.

Though he did intend to tell her about the message her dad left on his phone. He had decided not to call Rick back and handle it by simply telling Adley what her dad had said in his voice mail. It might be best not to engage Rick, even to tell him he wouldn't get involved.

By the time Nate was done showering and he'd thrown on a pair of blue jeans and a blue button-down shirt, rolled at the sleeve, a car was pulling into the driveway. It wasn't Adley and Grandpa, since they'd taken the pickup truck. This was a sleek BMW, and it wasn't hard to see who was driving.

Spencer Ford.

What was he doing here?

Nate stepped out onto the back porch to see what Spencer wanted. The sooner he could get him to leave, the better. He just hoped Spencer wasn't there to put more pressure on Adley to sell the farm.

Spencer parked his BMW by the toolshed. Strange. If he was just stopping by to see if Adley was home, why would he park his vehicle out of the way?

He got out of his car, wearing a pair of nice jeans and a suit coat. He glanced toward the barn and then to the house. His face tensed a little when he saw Nate. But he still put on a polished smile as he came across the driveway.

"Adley not home yet?" Spencer asked.

"Nope." Nate crossed his arms and planted his feet. "Can I help you?"

Spencer looked toward the road and shook his head. "Adley asked me to meet her here."

Nate wasn't sure why Adley would do something like that, but it wasn't his place to ask—as much as he'd like to.

"She mentioned needing some help today," Spencer continued. "She's been so overwhelmed, I wanted to ease her burdens in any way I could."

His words felt like a punch to Nate's gut. It was Nate who had been easing Adley's burdens for the past six weeks. Nate who had shown up way before today to meet her needs. Had Adley really asked this guy to step in now, when most of the hard work was done?

Anger and resentment flared to life, surprising Nate. He hadn't helped Adley for recognition or praise. He had come because his best friend had asked him, and he had stayed, because Adley and Benny and Grandpa Jed had needed him. But now? When Adley didn't seem as overwhelmed or stressed out, had she really asked Spencer to step in to relieve her burdens?

Nate's back was tense, and he lifted his chin. "Feel free to wait for her here. She should be home soon. I've got a few things to take care of."

"Need any help?"

"I've got it all under control." Nate left the porch, knowing he couldn't sit around and try to make small talk with Spencer. It wouldn't be good. There was too much tension and frustration building up inside Nate to make nice with the guy who might be replacing him when he left tomorrow.

Instead, he went to the barn where the tables and chairs were still waiting to be set up. The work was a good distraction until he saw another car pull into the driveway. The caterers would be arriving soon, bringing the appetizers and beverages. The band was also due to arrive any minute. They'd all need help setting up and getting ready for the Honeybee Ball, which started at seven.

Right behind the car were Adley and Grandpa Jed in their pickup truck.

More than anything, Nate wanted to wash his hands clean of the whole situation and let Spencer deal with everything. He'd been so eager to help, after all. But it was petty and childish. Nate knew where the outlets were for the caterers and how Adley wanted the band to set up on the north end of the barn. Things would run a lot smoother if Nate directed everyone.

No matter how he felt about Spencer, or how hurt he might be that he wasn't enough for Adley, he couldn't let her down now.

But he wasn't going to rush out of the barn—not yet.

Soon, another vehicle showed up with the band, and a large catering van pulled into the driveway. Steve and Paul were right behind them.

Adley was bombarded with people the moment she stepped out of the truck.

In no time at all, Steve and Paul made their way to the barn and started to help Nate set up the tables and chairs. The extra car had belonged to Ruthann from the inspection committee. She approached Adley and spoke to her with animation as she pointed to various parts of the farm.

Grandpa Jed walked over from the pickup and took a seat on a chair, near the barn door, directing traffic as best he could. He looked pleased and a little important as he caught Nate's eye.

"There you are," he said. "Was wondering where you were."

"Just working in here, trying to be as helpful as I can before I leave tomorrow."

Grandpa studied him for a long time. "You going to go through with it, then?"

"With what?"

"Leaving."

Nate glanced at Adley, who looked up at him. There was something new in her eyes—accusation? Anger?

He frowned. Why would she be angry at him? Nate was the one who had reason to be frustrated with her—not the other way around. He looked away, feeling his own anger rising.

"Yeah," Nate said. "First thing tomorrow. I'd go tonight if I didn't think I'd be needed to help clean up after the party."

Grandpa sighed. "That's a real shame. Having you here was like having a little bit of Benjamin return. I had missed you just about as much as I miss him."

Nate would have found Grandpa Jed's words warm and comforting if he hadn't been so upset.

Spencer approached Adley, and she offered him a wide smile. It twisted Nate's gut with jealousy, and he had to look away. Was something developing between them, like her parents had hoped? The way they looked at each other was a good indication that things were moving in that direction.

Wasn't that what Nate had thought Adley needed? Someone like Spencer? Then why did it feel so wrong?

With his back to the door, Nate didn't notice that Spencer had entered the barn until he almost bumped into him, carrying a large section of the dance floor.

"Sorry about that," Spencer said as he stepped back. "What can I do to help?"

Nate wanted to ignore him, but he was a better person than that—at least, that's what he liked to tell himself. "We need to get these floor pieces put down and locked together."

"Sure thing."

They worked side by side, but neither man said an unnecessary word to the other the whole time.

Adley kept busy, directing the caterers and band and anyone else who arrived to set up for the event. The Minnesota Association of Beekeepers sent a representative with a membership table, and the other grant finalists also needed space for their trifold displays with pictures of their farms and families for others to see.

But the most annoying part of Nate's day was whenever Spencer went out of his way to talk to Adley—and especially when he made her smile. Instead of giving him the same look of anger and accusation that she cast in Nate's direction, every time she glanced at Spencer, she always offered him a broad smile.

Nate's irritation and jealousy wound tighter and tighter.

What was wrong with him? He was acting like a middle schooler—but this time, he wouldn't sit back like he had so many years ago. As soon as Spencer left Adley's side, Nate approached her.

"Hey," he said, trying to cool his emotions so he didn't make the situation worse, but he suspected that his irritation still clouded his face and voice.

She glanced up at him, but she didn't smile. "Hey."

He wanted to ask her why she was angry at him, but this wasn't the time or place. They needed some privacy. "Can we talk?"

Adley was setting out samples of the Wilson honey, close to where the other finalists would put out their displays. She barely looked up at him. "Yeah." Her voice was full of an emotion he couldn't pinpoint. "We need to talk, but I've got too much to do right now."

He couldn't wait. He took a step closer to her

and lowered his voice, not wanting anyone else to hear. "Are you mad at me?"

"Did my dad talk to you about selling the farm?"

Nate frowned. "He called me, but—"

"Great. That's all I need is you telling me what to do with my life, too."

"Tell you what to do?" Nate's frown deepened. "I have no idea what you're talking about, Adley. I've never tried to tell you what to do."

"I don't have time for this right now. You can tell my dad that I'm not selling. Benny and I are doing just fine on our own. I don't need him— or you—to interfere in our life."

Her words hit him like a freight train, and he lifted his hands. "Fine. Consider me done here."

If he'd had any reservations about leaving before, they were gone. He had fulfilled his promise to Benjamin. She'd made it clear that he wasn't needed or wanted, and anyone could easily fill his shoes.

It was time for Nate to leave, and the sooner, the better.

# Chapter Thirteen

It didn't take Nate long to pack up his bags. The farm continued to buzz with activity as more and more people arrived to help Adley prepare for the ball. Vehicles clogged the driveway, trying to park in all sorts of random places. Someone should have been directing them to the field he had mowed earlier that day—but if it wasn't him, then it probably wouldn't get done.

Nate tossed his bags into the back of the pickup truck and sighed. No matter how angry he was, or how hurt he felt by Adley's words, he couldn't leave her with this mess.

He left his truck and went to the driveway, motioning for people to go to the field. He stopped to talk to several, sending them in the right direction. When it looked like the general flow of traffic was heading toward the proper parking area, he went back to his truck. Everything else was running fine. The tables and chairs were set up, the dance floor was laid down, the caterers were in place, and the band was warming up. Nate jumped into his pickup truck, ready to leave.

Adley's words still stung. She didn't want him interfering in her life. The last thing he wanted was to leave—especially like he had last time. No goodbyes, no well-wishes, no kind words to see him through the lonely days ahead. Nothing but anger and regret.

It was a lot like the last time.

Nate put his hands on the steering wheel and stared straight ahead, and that's when he noticed Grandpa Jed walking toward him. He was moving slowly, his face wincing in pain with each step he took.

It looked like this was a bad day for his arthritis.

Jumping out of the truck, Nate realized, belatedly, that he was going to leave without saying goodbye to Grandpa Jed—and Benny. Remorse filled him and he met the older man a few feet away from his truck.

"Help me in," Grandpa Jed said to Nate.

"Into the house?"

"Into your truck. You and I need to have a little chat, and we can't do it here."

Nate did as Grandpa Jed requested and helped him into his truck, then he got in himself.

"Take me to the lake, Nate," Grandpa said. "It's been too long since I've been there."

With all the activity going on around them, Nate hadn't expected Grandpa Jed to ask him to go to the lake, but he wasn't about to say no. He took one of the roads that led back to the beach. It was just as overgrown as the rest of the property had been when Nate showed up.

"You looked like you were fixing to leave us without saying goodbye," Grandpa Jed said. "Again."

The same remorse from before filled Nate's gut, but he didn't say anything as they bounced along the old, rutted road.

"I overheard your fight with Adley." Grandpa looked at Nate. "Sounds to me like you two need to have a good, long conversation."

Nate looked out at the field they were passing. "I think we're beyond that."

"No one is beyond a good conversation. You two have always struggled to say what needs to be said, and it's no wonder."

"Why?"

"You're scared out of your mind that you're going to lose her forever, which is the very thing that'll happen if you let your fear win. I think it's the thing that's been driving you since you were a teenager." He studied Nate. "You almost lost her for good the first time. You gonna let it happen a second time?"

They pulled up to the lake, and Nate put the truck in Park before he turned off the engine.

Memories assailed him here. Not just from the bachelor and bachelorette parties, or from the last time he was here with Adley, but from so many times swimming with Benjamin as teenagers. They had come here often, to cool off after work or to spend a lazy afternoon fishing with Grandpa Jed. The lake wasn't very big and sat within the Wilson family property, so there were no other houses or cabins. It was quiet and still. Just like Nate liked it.

Adley hadn't been wrong when she said that it had become overgrown. Earlier today, Nate had come here to clean it up to surprise her. Weeds had been growing along the shoreline, almost choking out the sandy beach. The logs they used to sit on were rotting and full of insects. Remnants of an old fire, several years old, had been in the firepit, encircled by rocks. And a tattered fishing boat was tangled up in the cattails. Nate had taken care of all of it.

"Well?" Grandpa Jed asked, not even looking at the lake or the beach. "Are you?"

Nate turned to meet Grandpa's gaze. "Nothing has ever come easily between Adley and me."

"I beg to differ. Your friendship is the easiest thing I've ever watched. You two work better together than most people I know." He hitched up his mouth as he shook his head. "The only thing that hasn't come easily to you is sharing your heart with her."

He spoke the truth, and Nate had to take in a deep breath. It had felt easier stepping off the airplane in Afghanistan to face his first deployment and the threat of warfare than it did to bare his heart to Adley Wilson.

"What's the worst thing that could happen?" Grandpa asked. "She rejected you once and it didn't kill you."

"No," Nate agreed ruefully, "but it was the hardest thing I've ever lived through—at least, until I watched Benjamin die."

"That's another thing," Grandpa said. "You need to forgive yourself where Benjamin's memory is concerned, son. What you did before his and Adley's wedding was wrong, but you've asked Adley for forgiveness and she's offered it, hasn't she?"

Nate nodded.

"Then all that's left is to forgive yourself.

You can't go back and change what happened four years ago—but that doesn't mean you can't make the future what you want it to be."

A loon floated by on the lake, calling out its echoing trill. Nate watched the beautiful black-and-white bird for a moment, thinking on Grandpa's words.

"You risk losing Adley," Grandpa conceded, "but you also might gain the greatest love story of your life. I see the way she looks at you, and I've been around long enough to know what it means. I can't tell you how she'll respond if you talk to her, but I can tell you that it's worth the risk."

"If she looks at me the way you claim," Nate said, "then why did she just tell me not to interfere in her life?"

"It's a defense mechanism she's had to develop over the past year. For quite a while now, it's been Adley against the world. She needs to believe she'll be just fine on her own—and she would be—but she also needs to realize that she might be better than fine with you at her side." Grandpa Jed put his hand on Nate's arm. "She's just as scared as you are, Nate."

The realization hit Nate hard. Adley was scared—just like him. He hated how fear had controlled so much of his life—it made him angry to think it might be controlling Adley's life, too. And not just where he was concerned, but in other areas, as well. An instinct to go to battle on her behalf overcame him. He had the most overwhelming desire to protect her and keep her safe from threats that he could see and those he couldn't. He hated to think of her fighting on her own. Though he knew her strength was one of her best qualities, she should use her energy to raise her son and build her business—not fight battles.

He couldn't leave her, not unless she truly wanted him to go. If that was the case, then he would honor her wishes and love her from afar. But if there was any spark of truth to Grandpa Jed's words, then he needed to stay and fight for her—for them.

But he wasn't going to do it now. Not tonight, not in front of everyone. She had enough to worry about with the ball and the grant ceremony. He'd learned his lesson the hard way four years ago. There was a right time and a wrong time to profess his love. And right now, if he barreled into the barn to tell her what was in his heart, like he had done so many years ago in this very spot, he would make a mess of things. Again.

"Grandpa?" Nate asked.

"Yeah?"

"I think I'm going to hang tight here for a while. I'd like to be alone, if you don't mind. Pull my thoughts together. I'll come up to the barn later, before the grant ceremony. But right now, if I show my face to Adley, it might make her more upset. She thinks I've left."

"You're probably right. If I know Adley, she needs some time to cool off before she can talk things through."

"Mind taking my truck back to the barn on your own? I'll walk back later."

"Don't mind at all."

Nate opened the door and hopped out.

Grandpa made his way around the truck and got into the driver's seat. He smiled at Nate. "I'll be praying for you," he said.

"Thanks." Nate would need all the prayers he could get if he was going to face his fears and confront the lies that had always prevented him from sharing his heart with Adley.

Grandpa Jed backed up the truck and turned it around, leaving Nate there by himself.

He walked to the edge of the lake and stared out at the glass-like water.

For as long as he could remember, probably since his dad had left, Nate had been afraid to open his heart up to be hurt again. His dad's abandonment and rejection had wounded him like nothing else, and the best way Nate had known to deal with the pain was to shove it inside and then not set himself up to feel it ever again. That's why he hadn't opened his heart to Adley all those years, and why he'd waited until the last minute to share his love with her. When she had rejected him, and rightly so, it had only confirmed his belief that it wasn't worth it to risk making himself vulnerable.

But now, as he stood on the cusp of doing it again, he realized the only way to true love, and real happiness, was taking the risk.

There was no other way.

Adley couldn't find a moment to herself to deal with the emotional storm brewing in her heart and mind. Instead of distracting her, the demands of the Honeybee Ball were just adding to her irritation and regret.

She had spoken to Nate in anger and fear, and had said things she wished she could take back. But he had left, and she was too busy to do anything about it.

When everything was finally in place and she had a moment to sneak away to change into her dress for the dance, she stood in front of the mirror in her bedroom and wanted to cry.

"Adley," she whispered to herself, shaking her head. "Why did you let him leave? Especially when you were angry?"

She had wanted to talk to him about what Spencer had said, but instead of discussing the accusations, she had made some of her own. And she had hurt him. She saw it in his face. After all he had done for her, she had said that she didn't want him interfering in her life. Nate could never be an interference. He had been a lifesaver, but she had made him feel like he had intruded. She owed him an apology, but now he was gone. Maybe for good.

Remorse filled Adley, and tears threatened to fall. She was alone again, and this time, it was her fault.

The band started to play in the barn, and Adley could hear the crunch of tires on the gravel below her open window. The bulk of the guests were arriving, and the dance had started. Later, Ruthann would make her announcement, and the grant would be given to one of the finalists.

Adley should have been excited. She should have been thrilled that her barn was filling up with her fellow beekeepers and that everything looked amazing. It had come together so beautifully, and she and Grandpa Jed had a lot to be proud of tonight.

But she didn't feel any of those things. All she felt was sadness and pain, knowing Nate was driving toward his new life in the Twin Cities, and she had probably ruined any chance they might have had to make a fresh start.

"Adley," Grandpa Jed called up to her. "People are asking for you."

"Coming." Adley used her curling iron to put a few waves into her long brown hair and touched up her makeup before putting on a pair of earrings. She hadn't dressed up like this in a long time and barely recognized herself in the mirror. The dress she had chosen had a patterned, long-sleeved blouse, gathered at the wrists, and a mid-length skirt that was chocolate brown. It complemented her hair and brought out the green of her eyes. She tucked one side of her hair behind her ear and let the other hang free.

Taking a deep breath, she slipped on her heels and left her room.

Grandpa Jed was waiting for her in the kitchen, and when she appeared at the bottom of the stairs his whole face lit up.

"You look as pretty as a picture, Adley Rae."

"Thank you, Grandpa."

He smiled. "I wish Nate was here to see you now. He wouldn't be able to take his eyes off you."

Adley's sadness deepened at the mention of

Nate. "He left, and I don't think he'll be coming back."

Grandpa Jed studied her face for a few seconds before saying, "Did you want him to leave?"

She shook her head as she pressed her lips together, already missing Nate more than she thought possible. Tears stung her eyes, and she went into Grandpa's embrace.

He held her tenderly. "It's okay," he said. "All is not lost."

It felt lost. *She* felt lost.

"Do you love him?" Grandpa Jed asked.

Adley did love Nate, with all her heart, and she wasn't afraid to admit it. "Yes."

"Then trust your love for him. Trust that if it's God's will, you and Nate will make it work."

The music coming in from outside reminded Adley that she had over a hundred people waiting for her in her barn. She couldn't appear to all of them with a red nose and puffy eyes. For tonight, she would have to put her personal issues aside and try to smile.

Adley pulled away from Grandpa, sniffing and looking for a tissue.

"Wipe your tears," Grandpa said, "and try to enjoy yourself tonight." He had a smile in his eyes that belied her fears. He appeared confident, and she wanted to feel confident, too, though she didn't. She wasn't so sure that everything would work out like he suggested.

After wiping her eyes and nose, she left the house with Grandpa.

Sommer was moving in and out of the crowd, her happy tail wagging at all the visitors. She loved people and kept dropping her tennis ball, hoping someone would pick it up and throw it for her.

"I'll put Sommer in her kennel," Grandpa said with a chuckle.

"She won't like that." Sommer was rarely in her kennel, usually having free rein of the property.

"We wouldn't want her to bother anyone tonight." He went off to gather up Sommer. It wasn't hard to get her into the kennel. All he had to do was throw her ball in there, and she followed it.

Adley walked into the barn, smiling, despite the heartache she felt.

She spoke to dozens of people, greeted the other finalists and made sure the caterers had everything they needed. She was just about to find Ruthann and the other committee members when Spencer came up to her side.

"Everything is amazing, Adley. Well done." A smile lit up his face. He was a handsome man—and kind. It was easy to like him.

"Thank you," she said. "I'm happy you could be here."

"So am I." He nodded to the dance floor where there were several couples dancing to a slow song. An air of gaiety filled the barn with people laughing, visiting and tapping their toes to the music. "Can I persuade you to dance with me?"

Adley didn't feel like dancing, but she didn't want to be rude, either. She could give him one dance, so she nodded.

He took her hand and led her to the dance floor. She put one hand on his shoulder and the other she kept clasped into his.

Spencer smiled down at her, but then his look shifted. "After I talked to you today, I had a chance to talk to your dad."

"Oh?" Adley followed his steps, finding it easy to dance with him. She didn't really want to talk about her dad, but he seemed intent on telling her what they had spoken about.

"I mentioned your surprise at what I had to say, that you didn't look or sound like you had agreed to sell the farm."

"I haven't—and I won't."

Spencer nodded, appearing to be a little disappointed. "I pressed him for the truth, and he finally admitted that you hadn't agreed, but that he was confident that if he could get Nate to persuade you, that you might."

"*If* he could get Nate to persuade me?"

"Yeah. That was the other part that he admitted, that he *hadn't* spoken to Nate yet but had left a message offering to pay him to help."

Adley's heart began to pound a little harder. "So Nate hasn't spoken to my dad about this yet?"

"Not that I'm aware of."

She had gotten angry at Nate for something he hadn't even done. It was just like her dad to perpetuate something like this—but she was the one who had fallen for it. She should have been smarter by now where her dad was concerned.

Adley shook her head as she looked at the barn around her and thought about how hard Nate had worked helping her achieve all of this—and he wasn't even there to enjoy it with her.

She couldn't hold her emotions in check any longer. She needed to call Nate's cell phone and ask him to come back—so she could apologize and they could talk.

"Will you excuse me?" Adley asked as she stopped dancing with Spencer. "I need to go find Nate."

Spencer's smile was sad but knowing. "It's Nate, huh?"

Adley nodded. "It's Nate."

He took a step back. "I hope you get everything your heart desires, Adley."

"Thanks, Spencer."

Adley turned away from Spencer, realizing she had set her phone down somewhere earlier today, but she couldn't remember where.

She tried to find it, but everywhere she looked, she found people who wanted to chat with her, instead.

"Are you looking for this?" Grandpa Jed appeared, holding up her phone, a smile on his face.

"Yes." She took it from him, looking to see if Nate had called or texted.

He hadn't.

"I'm going to call Nate and ask him to come back," she said as she started to unlock her phone.

Grandpa Jed put his hand over hers, and she looked up with a question on the tip of her tongue.

"He didn't leave, Adley."

Her pulse sputtered, and her breath stilled. "He didn't?"

"He's at the beach. We had a little chat, and he decided to hang out there and let the situation cool for a bit before he found you to talk."

A weightless wonder filled her stomach. "Nate's here?" She couldn't believe Grandpa hadn't told her, letting her wallow in her self-pity for over half an hour.

"He's down at the lake. Probably wouldn't mind a little visit from you, either."

Adley didn't wait for Grandpa to finish what he was saying.

She was determined to tell Nate she was sorry—and to tell him she loved him. Once and for all.

# Chapter Fourteen

Adley left behind the dance, the music, the food and the people. Here, at the back of the barn, facing the lake in the distance, the noise and the lights from the Honeybee Ball were muted. Crickets hummed in the tall grass, and the dark autumn sky was full of a million twinkling stars, dimmed only by the light of the brilliant harvest moon.

It was also cooler without the heat from the crowd in the barn. Adley wrapped her arms around herself as she picked her way over the rutted trail that led to the lake, her pulse thrumming through her veins. From here, she couldn't make out any of the shapes near the beach. Everything was silhouetted against the darkening sky, and it wasn't until she was closer to the water that she was able to discern where Nate was sitting.

He was on one of the logs, looking out at the lake. He didn't move and didn't appear to notice her arrival.

There was enough moonlight to see that the beach had been cared for recently. All the weeds were gone, the grass was mowed down and new logs were stacked by the firepit, waiting for a fire. Had Nate done this? She had a yearning to light the fire and sit here with Nate all evening, forgetting about all the people in the barn. Being alone with him was more appealing than all the Honeybee Balls in the world. He made her feel complete in a way that nothing and no one ever had. She felt the most like herself with Nate and had found herself increasingly craving those times when it was just the two of them.

Yet right now, with this big conversation facing her, she wasn't quite so excited. It could go wrong for so many different reasons, and that was the last thing she wanted.

She stood there for a moment, wondering how to even begin, when he suddenly turned and noticed her.

"Adley." He stood to face her, his back to the lake.

Her heart was beating so quickly, she was

afraid she might pass out before she could tell him what she needed to say.

"Why aren't you at the ball?" he asked.

"Grandpa Jed told me you were down here." She took a step closer to him, longing to take his hand and feel his strength and warmth. Instead, she stayed where she was standing, knowing she didn't deserve his love, not after the way she had treated him earlier. "I was going to call you and ask you to come back."

"You were?"

She took another step closer, wishing it were brighter outside and she could see his beautiful brown eyes better. Ever since she could remember, his eyes had made her feel safe, protected—special. He knew the real Adley and had still wanted to be part of her life. He had been her warrior and champion when they were younger, but he'd also been a confidant and a cheerleader, making her believe she was capable and strong and smart. She'd missed everything about him when he had been away, though her anger at him all those years had trumped her tender feelings.

But not anymore. She had finally come to a place in her life where she could recognize that despite the heartache she and Benjamin had lived through, they had loved each other and wanted the best for each other. If he had lived, they would have been happy and would have worked through their hardships. But he hadn't lived, and God had chosen a different path for Adley's life. Benjamin's death was the hardest thing she had ever endured, but if she would let God work through her, there could be redemption. There could be life after heartache and healing after pain.

Adley watched Nate now, wondering if her healing would include him. "I wanted you to come back so I could tell you I was sorry for what I said. Sorry I was angry at you. But especially sorry I let my dad get under my skin again and try to ruin a relationship that means more to me than any other."

He stayed on the other side of the log, making no move to come to her. She wished she knew what he was thinking. If she could only see his eyes, to read his emotions, she might not feel so cold and vulnerable right now.

She took a deep breath and walked closer to him—close enough that she could smell the cologne he was wearing and get a better view of his handsome face.

"I'm sorry, Nate," she said again. "For everything."

Gently, he reached up and tucked her hair

back behind her ear. His touch was sweet and tender, and though it was feather soft, she felt it all the way to her toes. It warmed her, despite the cold.

"I would forgive you a million times, Adley. You don't even need to ask."

He laid his palm against the side of her cheek and she placed her hand over his. Tears filled her eyes as she met his gaze. "I love you, Nate." She had to swallow the emotions clogging her throat. "The best thing that ever happened to me was the day you came back. I don't want you to leave again."

He placed his other hand on her other cheek and she stared back at him, hoping and praying he loved her, too, and that she hadn't missed her opportunity.

Nate could hardly breathe. The only things that felt real to him in this moment were Adley's cool cheeks beneath the palms of his hands. She was an anchor he had been desperately searching the world over for as the storms of his life blew him this way and that.

His heart was pounding so hard, he was afraid he hadn't heard her right. She said she loved him and she didn't want him to leave again.

It was in this very spot, on a much different

day, over four years ago, that he had been the one to tell her that he loved her. But here she was, opening her heart up to him in a way he had always hoped and prayed she would.

And he was speechless.

She stared at him, her green eyes large and bright, filled with so many different emotions, he couldn't keep track. But it was the fear he saw there—possibly the fear of what he might say—that made him finally find his voice, if for no other reason than to banish that fear forever.

"I love you, too, Adley. I've loved you for as long as I've known you. I couldn't possibly know you and not love you." His words felt a little breathless, but he had said them.

The fear in her eyes disappeared, and they filled with a light he had never seen before. Awe radiated from her face.

Nate couldn't let anything else stand between them, so he stepped over the log and pulled Adley into his arms, needing to feel her as close as possible to still his racing pulse.

But it only made his senses become more alive.

She clung to him, burying her face in his neck. He could feel her heart pounding against his—or possibly it was his own heart beating so hard. He wasn't sure. All he knew was that nothing had ever felt as right as this moment, with Adley in his embrace.

When she pulled back to look at him, he smiled, wanting nothing more than to kiss her. It's what he had dreamed about more times than he could count.

She returned the smile, a little bashful. She looked so pretty in her dress, with her hair curled and earrings dangling from her ears. In his mind, she had never looked lovelier than she did right now.

Slowly, allowing her time to respond, he lowered his lips to hers.

She met his kiss with an eagerness that matched his own. She was sweet and gentle as she kissed him back.

He pulled her tighter, all of his muscles responding to her nearness and the tenderness in her lips. He'd never, in all of his imaginings, known that kissing her would feel this wonderful. She melded against him perfectly, as if she'd been carved from him and had now found her way back to her rightful home.

He could have kissed her all night, but the muted noise of the ball returned him to his senses and he pulled back, already looking forward to finding himself in this position again.

"We still have so much to talk about," Adley

said to him. "So many things to discuss and decide."

"It's safe to say that I know exactly what I want," he said with a smile.

"What do you want, Nate?"

"I want you, and Benny, and even Grandpa Jed, for as long as I can have you. I don't want to leave the farm, or your side, ever again."

She smiled, reaching up and tracing the ridge of his cheekbone with her finger, driving him nearly to distraction. "That sounds an awful lot like what I want."

He kissed her again. He couldn't help it. And she fell back into his embrace as if she'd always been there.

When she finally pulled away, and his chest had begun to rise and fall with a steady rhythm again, he said, still having a hard time believing all this was happening, "Will you marry me, Adley?"

Slowly, she nodded, and then finally, as if trying to gather her emotions together long enough to respond, she said, "I will."

He lifted her into the air and spun her—he couldn't help it. He'd never felt such a jolt of energy or happiness in his life. Then he brought her back down to press against his chest, and hugged her like he'd never hugged anyone else before.

She laughed and wrapped her arms around his neck. "You make me feel young again, as if anything and everything is possible."

"You are young," he countered. "And everything *is* possible, Adley. I've never felt so empowered before as I do right now. I'm in awe that God brought us back together and has given me the desires of my heart."

Her smile was bright, and so sweet, he was tempted to kiss her again—but he refrained, knowing they needed some time to talk.

"You are an answer to prayer, Nate," she said. "And the most amazing blessing and gift to me and Benny and Grandpa Jed." She paused and studied him. "You don't mind that Grandpa Jed is part of the picture?"

"Mind?" Nate laughed and shook his head. "If he wasn't already living here, I would ask if he could. He's been more of a father and grandfather to me than my own."

Adley put her hands on either side of Nate's face and gave him a kiss. "Thank you," she said. "For loving him like I love him."

She sighed and lowered her hands. "I suppose we should get back to the dance. They'll be announcing the grant winner soon—and since I'm technically hosting this event, I should probably be there."

He smiled and nodded, taking her hand in his as they started to walk back to the barn.

It felt good and right to be holding Adley's hand. He couldn't help but think of all those years he had watched her from a distance, hoping and praying that she would return his love. It was almost too good to be true, but he remembered what Pastor Dawson had said last week at church, that God was in the business of giving good gifts to His children.

Adley wrapped her fingers around his and drew close to his side, holding his arm with her other hand, as if she couldn't get close enough.

He placed his free hand over hers, loving how it felt to be touched by her. To be loved and wanted.

"Adley," he said gently, "I want you to know that I loved Benjamin like a brother."

She was quiet for a moment, but then she said, "I know. And he loved you, too."

"I never wanted to hurt him, or you. I want to always honor his memory with you, Benny, Grandpa and the farm."

"Does that mean you want to stay on the farm and keep running it?"

He looked down at her. "I never thought otherwise."

"What about your marketing business?"

"I'll run that on the side—but the farm will always come first."

"Thank you, Nate."

"I want this farm to be the best it can be so that one day, if Benny wants to take on the family business and continue the legacy, it will be better than ever before."

"He'll have more than one legacy to continue," she said. "The Wilson legacy and the Marshall legacy. How many boys are blessed enough to have two strong men to call Father? Even if he never had a chance to meet the first?"

"He'll know Benjamin as well as I did," Nate promised. "I'll make sure of that."

"I know you will."

They were almost to the barn when Nate paused, noticing another vehicle as it pulled into the farmyard. The driver didn't park with the other cars but came to a stop in the most inconvenient location outside the barn.

"I forgot my parents were coming with Benny," Adley said. "I asked them to be here when the grant was announced. My mother said she'd put Benny to bed after that and sit with him while I finished up the night. I missed him and wanted him to wake up at home tomorrow morning."

Nate's stomach knotted at the sight of Rick Johnson stepping out of his Porsche in his slick suit.

In all the joy of the previous moments, he had forgotten about Adley's dad. Just thinking about the confrontation they were going to have, and all the horrible things Rick might say, made Nate's muscles tense up.

Yet Adley and Benny were worth every insult Rick could hurl at him.

They would always be worth the fight.

# Chapter Fifteen

Adley took a deep breath as she and Nate stepped into the light from the barn. She still clung to Nate's arm and had no intention of letting go. They were in for a fight with her father, but she wouldn't let her dad insult the man she loved and intended to marry.

Dad closed his car door while he inspected the barn, not noticing Adley and Nate.

Mom stepped out and immediately went to the back seat to remove Benny and his car seat. It was past his bedtime, and he was probably sleeping. If he was, Adley had no wish to wake him. She just missed him and wanted him home with her. Two nights at her parents' house was far too many.

Nate's muscles clenched under Adley's hands, and she looked up to meet his gaze. The light from the barn allowed her to finally see his eyes, and when she did, she saw the love he had for her, mingled with the apprehension he must be feeling at seeing her dad.

"We don't have to talk to them tonight," Adley said to Nate, starting to pull away. Though everyone was in the barn and wouldn't hear them, she didn't want to force Nate to have this discussion while the ball was in full swing. "We can wait to have this conversation later, when we're alone."

He held tight to her hand. "I'm tired of letting your dad dictate who I am and how I am supposed to feel. He's the reason I didn't tell you how I felt about you when we were young."

"My dad was?" Adley frowned. "What do you mean?"

"Remember our eighth-grade winter formal? When I asked you to dance with me?"

Adley nodded, remembering it well. She even smiled. "I was so happy that you finally asked me to dance. I had been crushing on you for months."

It was his turn to look confused. "You had a crush on me?"

"You don't have to sound so surprised. Of course I had a crush on you. Most of the girls in our grade did. You were the best-looking, the most athletic and a little bit of a bad boy. Who wouldn't have liked you?"

He smiled down at her, giving her a look that she felt all the way to her toes.

"When you asked me to dance," Adley went on, "I thought you were going to tell me you liked me. After the dance, you left the gym, and all my friends came up to me, giggling and teasing me. They all agreed and thought you liked me, too. But when you came back into the gym, you completely ignored me for the rest of the dance. And it was a long time before you even talked to me again. After that, we were just friends. Until the day before my wedding to Benjamin, I had no idea how you really felt."

Nate swallowed and glanced up at her dad again. He was helping Mom get Benny's diaper bag out of the back seat. "Your dad was chaperoning the dance, remember? When I went into the hallway to get a drink from the water fountain, and to get up the courage to tell you how I felt, he cornered me." The pain in his eyes made Adley want to weep. He almost looked like an thirteen-year-old again. "It was dark and he was so big, I've never been more scared in my life. He told me to stay away from you, said I wasn't good enough for you and I had no business even being your friend."

Embarrassment and revulsion churned in Adley's stomach. "My dad?" she whispered.

Nate didn't even bother to nod or acknowledge her question. "I'm sorry I let him win, Adley."

"You're sorry?" Adley's heart broke for Nate. "He was a grown man and you were a child." Her voice caught. "You have nothing to be sorry about, Nate. I'm the one who's sorry—sorry I didn't realize what was happening. He's my dad. I should have protected you from him."

"You didn't know." He put his hand up to her cheek. "I didn't want you to know. He *is* your dad, and I didn't want you to think less of him. My dad skipped out on us—at least you had your dad. I would have given almost anything, and put up with almost anything, to have him be a part of my life."

She studied Nate's dear face, admiring his strength and courage. "You are going to make an incredible father to Benny."

He gently kissed her upturned face.

When he pulled back, Adley looked toward her parents and found them staring wide-mouthed at her and Nate.

She took a deep breath to fortify herself for the fight they were about to have. But she didn't want it near the barn, in case one of her guests would step out and hear them. Instead of letting her parents come to her, she and Nate walked toward them.

They were far enough away from the barn that they would have a bit of privacy.

Nate still held Adley's hand as they approached her parents.

Dad stared hard at Nate.

Mom recovered quickly and removed all emotions from her face, slipping her company mask into place. She offered Adley a smile. "Hello, dear. Benny's been almost perfect. He's sleeping now, so I thought I might sneak into the house and put him to bed and then join you all in the barn with the video monitor for the announcement. We haven't missed it, yet, have we?"

"It's supposed to be announced at eight."

"Oh, good, then I'll have time." She started to move toward the house, but Adley stopped her.

"Mom, can you please stay for a minute? Nate and I have something to say."

Dad was still staring at Nate without saying a word.

Mom glanced at Dad with uncertainty and then nodded. She still held Benny in his car seat, though Benny was sound asleep.

Adley pressed closer to Nate and looked up at him, drawing strength from his presence and his love. He nodded encouragement at her.

"Nate and I are getting married," Adley said to her parents. "We're going to stay on the farm and keep running it for Benny."

Her parents were quiet for a moment, and then her mom set Benny's car seat down and gave Adley a hug. "Congratulations, dear. I'm happy if you're happy." She looked at Nate and smiled at him. "Welcome to the family, Nate."

"Thank you," he said as he turned his wary gaze toward Adley's dad. He lifted his chin, just enough to suggest strength but not defiance. "Mr. Johnson, I know I didn't get a chance to talk to you first, but I hope Adley and I have your blessing. I love your daughter more than life itself. I've loved her for a long time, and I know I'll love her for the rest of my life."

No one spoke for a moment as Rick crossed his arms. Adley had seen that stance before and knew it didn't bode well for what he was going to say, so Adley spoke first.

"Dad, I love you." She took a deep breath. "But you've tried to manipulate and control everyone around you for as long as I've been alive. I want you to be a part of our lives, but if you can't honor our love and our future marriage, then you can't be involved. I'm an adult now, and I know what I want and who I want to spend my life with." She looked up at Nate, who was watching her closely. "I've never met a more honorable or selfless man than Nate Marshall. I consider myself blessed that he would still love me, despite the past." She returned her gaze to her father. "But he does—and I love him. We will be married, no matter how upset that might make you. And we will stay on this farm, no matter how much money we could make by selling. This is my final decision, and now you have a choice to make. Either accept what I've said or watch from a distance."

Mom pleaded with Dad with her eyes. She went back to Benny and lifted his car seat, holding it close, as if she wasn't about to give him up.

Dad took in the scene, looking from Adley to her mom to Nate. He was an intelligent man, so Adley hoped he was smart enough to realize this decision held more importance than almost all the others he'd made where she was concerned.

Finally, he let out a sigh, his jaw clenched. He didn't look happy, but he nodded. "I won't say a word against either of you," he said. "It's not what I would have chosen for you, Adley, but you are old enough to make your own choices."

It wasn't a blessing, but it was a start.

Adley let out her own sigh, wishing things

could be different between her and her father. It wasn't for lack of trying on her part. Maybe one day, he would find a way to be happy for her.

"They're going to announce the grant winner soon," Adley said. "We should get back to the dance."

"I'll run Benny up to his room," Mom said.

Dad didn't say a thing as Adley and Nate walked away from them and toward the barn.

"Thank you for standing up to him," Nate said. "I know it isn't easy."

"No, but it was necessary." She smiled at him. "We're a team now. It's not just you or me against the world. We'll do it all together."

He returned her smile. "I love you."

"I love you, too."

They entered the barn, hand in hand, and found Grandpa Jed.

His grin lit up the room, and he gave both of them a tight hug. "Are you getting hitched?" he asked.

Adley nodded. "As soon as possible."

Nate looked at her. "I'm ready whenever you are."

Grandpa laughed. "You'll stay here, won't you?"

"If you'll have us," Adley said.

"This home is yours—both of yours." Grandpa

squeezed Adley's free hand. "I couldn't be happier for the two of you."

"Thank you." Adley's heart warmed, and she was so thankful for Grandpa Jed and his unconditional love. It covered over the pain of her father's disapproval.

The band finished the song it was playing, and Ruthann took one of the microphones.

"If I can have your attention," she said.

Everyone quieted and turned their focus to the front of the barn.

Adley's pulse picked up a steady hum, but Nate's presence beside her made her feel calm.

"First, I would like to thank the Wilson family for hosting this event. Everything is beautiful, and you've been so welcoming. Thank you."

Everyone clapped, and Grandpa lifted his hand to acknowledge them.

When the applause died down, Ruthann said, "Earlier today, we announced the three finalists for the Minnesota Association of Beekeepers grant and the Minnesota Honeybee Farm of the Year award. I had the honor of visiting the finalists and their farms this past month, with two other committee members. We judged the farms with a set of criteria that you can find on our website. I think it goes without saying that each farm is unique and wonderful in its own right. We are blessed to have such amazing beekeepers in Minnesota, and I wish there was an award for everyone."

There was more applause.

Adley was trying to keep her emotions in check as she waited for Ruthann to announce the winner.

"Even if we don't win," Nate whispered to Adley, "we'll be fine. We'll work hard to keep up the momentum we've started this past fall and continue to grow."

She smiled at him, believing him with all her heart. They were a good team, and she had nothing but hope for the future.

But she still wanted to win.

"Without further ado," Ruthann said into the microphone, "I would like to announce this year's winner." She opened an envelope and smiled. "The winner of the Minnesota Honeybee Farm of the Year award, and the grant, go to Jedediah Wilson and Adley Wilson."

Applause erupted, and Adley's chest expanded with delight.

Nate let go of her hand and motioned for her and Grandpa to go up and receive the award.

But Adley reached for Nate's hand again and tugged him along with her.

"You're the reason we won," she said to him. "And you deserve this as much as Grandpa Jed and me."

He smiled at her and nodded.

Adley couldn't wait to share everything with him.

The day was bright and warm, much warmer than normal for the last weekend in October. Nate stood at the front of the barn, Pastor Dawson on one side, a buddy from the Guard acting as his best man on the other. Nate felt calm—much calmer than he had imagined when he had thought about his wedding day.

But it wasn't hard for him to realize why. This felt right—like the most natural thing he'd ever done before. He was marrying Adley today. She was his best friend, his biggest cheerleader, and the woman he respected and admired more than anyone else on earth.

Mom sat in the front row, a tender smile on her face as she met Nate's gaze and slowly shook her head back and forth, in both wonder and amazement. When Nate and Adley had invited her out to the farm to tell her the news, she'd been shocked, but had quickly accepted their decision and become their biggest supporter. She latched on to Benny as if he'd always been her grandson, and she'd made herself comfortable at the farm, stopping by often to visit and help plan the wedding.

Adley and Mom got along well, which made Nate grateful. If she still thought Adley was too good for her son, she didn't say so, or even behave that way anymore. She was proud to call Adley her daughter, and prouder still of the man her son had become—and she told him that often.

The barn was filled with white chairs on either side of an aisle that Adley would soon walk down. Dozens of friends and family filled the space, their smiling faces looking at Nate in expectation and happiness. He returned their smiles, willing the clock to turn over, impatient to see his bride, who would be walking in on her father's arm at any moment.

Rick hadn't said one word against Nate or their impending wedding, but neither had he been involved in the planning. He had come that morning, with his wife, and had stood by, watching as preparations unfolded around him. At the appointed hour, he had gone into the house—for the first time—and was there with Adley now.

Nate wished he could be there with her, protecting her, if need be, hoping and praying that healing was taking place and that when they appeared, it would be with joy on both their faces.

As for Benny, he was sitting on Grandpa Jed's lap, near Nate's mom. The baby was content to play with Grandpa's pocket watch as he giggled and craned his neck to look at all the strange people on his farm.

Nate's chest expanded at the sight of the baby, marveling that he would have the honor of being Benny's father. It was a privilege he would never take for granted, striving each day of his life to be the man Benny—and Benjamin—needed him to be. For the baby, and for Adley.

The music changed and the violinist began to play "Canon in D." Nate's pulse picked up speed as he looked over the tops of everyone's heads and saw Adley approaching the barn on her father's arm.

His breath caught at the sight of her. If he was asked later what her gown looked like in that moment, or what color her flowers were, he wouldn't be able to answer. All he would remember from that first glance was the look of love that radiated from her face as her gaze found his. She was lovelier than any other woman he'd ever known, and she was his, all his, for as long as he walked on the earth. Adley was going to be his wife, for better or worse, for richer or poorer, in sickness and in health, for as long as they both would live. It was a mystery he struggled to understand, but instead of trying to grasp something so profound, he decided to bask in the glory of God's perfect design.

As she drew closer, he took in her long flowing gown, with the satin and lace, the loose sleeves, gathered at the wrists, and the simplicity of her hair, which she wore down around her shoulders like a veil. She had chosen not to wear anything on her head but had tucked one side of her hair behind her ear. She was the most beautiful bride he'd ever seen.

When she came to a stop, near where Nate was waiting, it was then that Nate glanced at her father.

Rick was eyeing up Nate with his usual gruff exterior. But when Rick looked at Adley, his eyes watered, and for a second, his tenderness was unmistakable. Before Nate was able to process the emotion, Rick straightened his back, giving off an air of indifference.

But for that brief moment, Nate saw what Rick didn't want anyone else to see. He was vulnerable where Adley was concerned, because of his great love for her. He hid his emotions behind an impenetrable facade, but they were there, and Nate had a bit more respect for his soon-to-be father-in-law.

When Rick offered Adley's hand to Nate, Nate spoke to Rick, for only his and Adley's ears to hear. "I will guard her heart and her life with all the strength and love I possess."

For a heartbeat, Rick looked at Nate, but then he softened—by only a degree—and nodded. "See that you do."

And then he stepped back, and Adley moved to Nate's side. She looked up at him with respect and love and mouthed the words "thank you."

"Dearly beloved," Pastor Dawson said as he looked out at the congregation. "We are gathered here today to witness the joining of two hearts, two families and two lives. Today, Adley Wilson and Nate Marshall will begin their married life together, and they have asked us to witness their vows. Marriage is a sacred union between the couple and God, but it is supported and sustained by friends and family. Let's begin with a word of prayer."

Nate entwined his fingers through Adley's, and she held on to him with a grasp that told him she would not let go any time soon.

"You're breathtaking," he whispered to her, just before Pastor Dawson began the prayer.

Her smile made his knees weak.

When he was done, Pastor Dawson began his sermon about the holy sanctity of marriage.

All Nate was aware of was Adley's presence at his side. Pleasure and longing stirred through him, and he could hardly believe that this day had finally arrived.

"Nate," Pastor Dawson said, "please repeat after me."

Nate turned to face Adley and took her other hand in his, smiling at her, admiring her strength and beauty. Joy radiated from her beautiful green eyes as she returned the look, gazing up at him with eagerness and bashfulness mixed together. He repeated the words Pastor Dawson said, and then it was Adley's turn. She also waited for Pastor Dawson's prompts, smiling at Nate the whole time.

"Do you have the rings?" Pastor Dawson asked Nate's best man.

He nodded and took them out of his pocket. They were simple gold bands with nothing flashy or fancy about them. They were a symbol of the ordinary days and nights that would fill Adley's and Nate's lives, banding together to make something valuable and strong, something that would not be easily broken, but would be beautiful.

They had chosen to speak their own vows, and so when Pastor Dawson handed Nate the first ring, and Nate slipped it onto Adley's finger, he said, "Adley, there is nothing in this world that is more precious or valuable to me than you. Ever since I was a boy, you've made me want to be the best version of myself. I don't always meet that goal, but I promise to you that I will keep it at the forefront of my choices and actions. Today, before all these witnesses, I am vowing to love you and honor you with all my heart, with all my mind and with my whole body. From this day forward, I will not think only of myself, but of you and Benny, and of any other children God might bless us with in the years ahead. This ceremony represents the beginning of something new and lasting, and with this ring, I thee wed." He ran his thumb over the ring as it came to rest on her finger.

Adley bit her bottom lip, and he saw that it was trembling. She took Nate's ring and slipped it onto his finger. "Nate, from the moment we met, you've been one of my best friends. Your strength, courage and fortitude have always impressed me, and the loyalty and devotion you have for the people you love is one of your shining qualities. I feel blessed and honored to be among those that you love. I want nothing more in life than to continue to grow the special relationship God has given us, for as long as He allows. I promise to love you, honor you and respect you from this day forevermore. With this ring, I thee wed."

"By the power vested in me by God and the state of Minnesota, I now pronounce you husband and wife." Pastor Dawson closed his Bible and smiled at the bride and groom. "You may kiss your bride, Nate."

Nate had kissed Adley several times since the night of the Honeybee Ball, but never had he kissed her as his wife. When he drew her into his arms and placed a gentle kiss upon her lips, as her husband, he was filled with a profound sense of wonder. Adley Marshall was his wife, his better half, his partner and his best friend. He marveled at how perfect she fit into his embrace and how much he loved her.

When they finally parted, to the cheers and laughter of their friends and family, Adley looked up at Nate, a secret smile on her lips.

"What?" he asked, meeting her gaze.

"Don't tell the others, but I have the best husband in the world."

He laughed and kissed her again.

"I'll keep your secret, if you're willing to keep mine," he whispered into her ear.

"What is your secret, Mr. Marshall?"

"I have the best wife in the world."

"Then it seems we're the perfect match."

And they were.

\* \* \* \* \*

Dear Reader,

Here in Minnesota, we have a rich heritage of farming. As of 2021, there are nearly 11,000 Century Farms recognized by the Minnesota State Fair Century Farm program. According to www.mda.state.mn.us, there are 3,470 dairy farms in the state, producing 9.5 billion pounds of milk. In contrast, according to www.minnesotagrown.com/honey there are only 96 honeybee farms, but they produce 7 million pounds of honey (only 5% of the United States output). I suppose it's safe to say that Minnesota is a land flowing with milk and honey. It was fun to write a story set on a honeybee farm. I was not raised on a farm and only visited them periodically over the course of my life, but they've always intrigued me. It's such a unique yet time-honored way of life. I loved researching honeybee farming for this story and hope I've done it justice.

Blessings,
*Gabrielle Meyer*